THE DETERMINED GROOM

The Hawk Brothers Romances #1

CAMI CHECKETTS

COPYRIGHT

The Determined Groom: The Hawk Brothers Romances #1

Cover art: Novak Illustrations

Editing: Daniel Coleman, Julia Lance, and Jenna Roundy

CHAPTER ONE

Emmett Hawk, former wide receiver for the Texas Titans, stood on the porch of the main cabin, waiting uneasily for the new batch of fitness camp attendees. This was round four of six of his week-long sports and fitness camps, and it was the first one for adults. The first two weeks had been filled with different ages of college-hopeful youth groups, and last week had been college athletes. Each group of twenty had been fun, yet challenging. This group was looking to be a flop. He'd hardly dealt with any cancellations with his other groups, but this week he'd had fifteen dropouts, for various odd reasons, and the camp hadn't even started yet. Five attendees.

He supposed it should bug him to spend a week on only five people, but what else did he have to do this summer? He smiled grimly. The fitness camp would still serve its purpose: giving *him* some kind of purpose. When he'd returned for spring ball after ripping out his ACL, MCL, PCL, and meniscus at the all-star game in February, the offensive coach and his head coach had sat him down and asked him to take a year off, see if he could heal and return to full strength. It was all a façade, a way to pretend he was coming back. He'd seen the truth in their eyes. They'd already replaced him. Nobody wanted a player who'd never be at full strength again. The media would have a heyday with the billionaire football player washed up after one season. Especially since he was a Hawk—he and his brothers were hounded by the media. Emmett didn't like it, but he tried his best to represent his family well.

Emmett was one of four brothers who would inherit the Hawk Dynasty. His grandfather had started with good old Texas oil and his father had expanded to worldwide real estate, everything from storage units to exclusive resorts like the one he was standing on. He looked around, drinking in miles of trees, a man-made lake, and a massive lodge in the middle of the property with wood-chipped trails throughout the forest and twenty individual cabins. He liked this resort and was grateful his brother Callum, who managed all of their commercial real estate, agreed to his idea, blocked out the summer for his fitness camps, and added a state-of-the-art training facility.

The shuttle van pulled up, and Emmett straightened his shoulders and plastered on his media smile. His assistant, Tracy, jumped out of the driver's seat of the van and waved. "Hey, boss."

He waved back. She was a top fitness trainer and really dressed the part, always in a tank top and spandex shorts with her dark hair pulled up in a ponytail.

Two teenagers who worked for the resort opened the van door and then hurried to go get the suitcases out. They were paid well to be courteous and instructed not to take tips. Emmett didn't want his attendees to be worried about carrying dollar bills around; he wanted them focused on improving their health and stamina.

Emmett strode down the stairs to meet them.

A leggy blonde slid out of the van first. She grinned Emmett's direction, and he instinctively backed up a step, swallowing hard. Oh no. Some of the female college athletes had been a little aggressive and too flirtatious with him, but he could sense this woman, a renowned supermodel, knew exactly how to push and was used to getting results with any man she set her sights on.

Behind her, a thin, fit middle-aged woman climbed out and stretched. "Oh, my aching butt," she said.

Emmett couldn't help but laugh.

She glanced up at him quickly. "Someday you'll be old too, so quit mocking me." She winked, but it was friendly, nothing like the sultry look the blonde was giving him as she slithered his way.

A young, burly guy with a shaved head climbed out. His face was stony, and he was well built. He must be one of *those*—tough NFL hopeful who had something to prove. He'd either soften his pride and learn from Emmett and the trainers this week, or he'd be trying so hard to claim he was tougher than Emmett he'd waste the entire experience.

A lean, tall guy with dark curls springing everywhere bee-bopped out. He turned quickly and offered his hand to whoever was behind him.

The supermodel was fast approaching, but Emmett shifted to the side so he could see the number five attendee. Dressed in a casual knit knee-length gray dress that clung to her in just the right way, the woman who stepped from the van looked like his version of an angel—her hair was dark and curly and hung down her back, her face was tan and smooth with high cheekbones and dark brows, and her eyes were a surprising bright blue that took his breath away.

When she smiled at the young man helping her, Emmett took an unconscious step forward and ran into the supermodel. *Crap.*

She grasped his forearm. "Emmett Hawk." She drawled out his name and her tongue darted out to moisten her lips. "I've been waiting a long time to meet you."

Emmett stepped back out of her reach but forced himself to extend his hand. "Nice to meet you, Miss ..."

She wrapped his hand up with both of hers and batted her long, spider-leg-looking eyelashes. "Britney Pearl. You've probably seen me. Cover of *Sports Illustrated* swimsuit edition last year."

Emmett pulled his hand free. "Congrats." Someone had shown him that cover in the locker room, but he hadn't lingered. His best friend from high school had become addicted to pornography, and it had recently ruined his marriage and his life. Emmett steered clear of women who thought their bodies were only to be used as a weapon to mess with men's minds.

He stepped past her and stuck his hand out to the fun middle-aged lady with highlighted brown and gold hair and obvious Spanish ancestry. She also had fake eyelashes, but they were tastefully done. She was pretty and fit.

"Emmett Hawk," he said. "Thanks for coming."

She grinned. "It's great to meet you." She shook his hand and released it, patting his cheek like his mom would do. "I'm Nana Lucy, or you can call me Cookie Nana," she said with a faint Spanish accent.

He matched her smile. "You bake a lot of cookies?"

"Yes, honey child, I sure do. But I guess that's not happening this week."

"No, ma'am, this week we'll be eating healthy and working hard."

She pulled a face. "And to think I liked you when I first saw you."

"We'll make fitness fun," he promised.

"I bet you make everything fun," Britney purred next to his elbow.

Emmett forced a smile and stepped quickly the other direction, sticking his hand out to the burly, surly guy. "Emmett Hawk."

The guy grasped his hand and squeezed. Emmett didn't roll his eyes, though he wanted to. He squeezed back until the guy winced and let go. "Troy Jones." The guy glared at him like he should be intimidated.

"Nice handshake." Emmett arched an eyebrow and moved on to the curly-haired guy, his excitement mounting that the gorgeous brunette was next.

The curly-haired guy had his hand out. "Gunner Travers. It's so cool to meet you, sir."

Emmett grinned. "You too. I think I'm only a couple years older than you, though, so none of this 'sir' business."

Gunner had deep dimples and his dark eyes sparkled. Emmett was sure the women all fell for him. "The 'sir' is because of my respect for your game, not your age, sir."

Emmett liked him already. "I appreciate that. You'll be a senior at Florida State?" Emmett already knew a little of his attendees' backgrounds, and he wished he hadn't asked the courtesy question so he could move on to the natural beauty to Gunner's right. Gunner and Troy were both going into their senior year. They should've come with the college crowd but had been at NFL recruiting events last week. They were both NFL hopefuls who wanted to push themselves to their peak fitness for their senior year of college.

"Yes, sir. Troy and I are getting rings this year for sure and both signing fat contracts with the NFL." He grinned confidently.

"I hope you do."

Emmett sidestepped once again, and all the positive feelings he'd had for Gunner dissipated as the young man placed his hand on the angel's back and she smiled sweetly up at him. "This is Cambree Kinley," Gunner said. "Elite Warrior racer, sixth-grade teacher, Colorado native, and the most beautiful woman in the world."

Cambree laughed easily. Her tinkling laughter was as pretty as the rest of her. She shook her head slightly at Gunner and muttered, "Flatterer," before stepping up to Emmett and putting her hand out. "Hi."

Emmett caught a breath as her hand fit into his like it was made to be there. She glanced sharply up at him, her smile disappearing as she studied him with those bright blue eyes.

"Happy to meet the most beautiful woman in the world," Emmett said, hoping it came across as teasing and not creepy.

She found her smile again. "Gunner's being a goofball. I already told him on the ride from the airport that I'm not into one-week flings, but he's set on proving me wrong."

Emmett decided he was going to thrash Gunner before the week was over. "I hope you stay strong, Miss Kinley."

"Don't worry. I'm the strongest chick I know."

Emmett couldn't resist looking over the lean form revealed

by her simple dress. She might be right. He liked how brutally honest she was. "This week will make you stronger."

"I worked six months to get here; it had better rock my world." She gave him a challenging look, and he planned on pushing her to her limit and enjoying being right there with her.

He had four other trainers on staff, so everybody was getting one-on-one training at this camp. Cambree Kinley was going to get his undivided attention this week, and maybe he could beat Gunner out of the contest for a one-week fling.

No. Cambree wasn't the type you had a fling with; she was too pure and intriguing. And he couldn't risk falling for a camp attendee when he needed to prove to himself, his dad, and the world that these fitness camps were a brilliant concept and a career as viable as the NFL. His stomach sank. Nothing was as great as playing football.

She pulled her hand back and glanced around. "This is incredible."

"Not as pretty as Colorado."

She smiled. "No. But don't take it personally. It's not your fault you have no mountains."

"We have something even better than mountains." He liked bantering with her.

"Oh yeah?" She elevated an eyebrow. "What's that?"

"Texas pride."

"I've heard about it. Can't wait to finally watch some Texas pride in action." She winked, all cute and sassy. Emmett's mouth went dry.

"Are we going to flirt or get to work?" Troy said drily.

"Shut up, I'm enjoying this," Lucy interjected.

Emmett glanced around to find that the entire group, plus his assistant Tracy and the other three trainers, watching the two of them. Britney was glaring at Cambree, and Emmett could feel the jealousy radiating off the swimsuit model. Yuck. He hated spiteful women.

He hurried to introduce the other trainers to everyone and then let Tracy direct them to their cabins to get settled in before they got to work. He watched Cambree go, admiring the striations in her calves. With only five attendees this week, he'd been able to do a little research on each of them. She was one of the elite Warrior women racers in the nation, and he thought it was equally as impressive that she could handle a class full of sixth graders.

Warrior races were gaining in popularity, and he'd been able to watch her compete in a few that had been posted on the internet. He'd thought she was attractive then, but she was blowing his mind in person.

It would be fun to push her physically, but he was even more excited about getting to know her better. She glanced over her shoulder at him, and his face burned as he realized he'd been caught staring. He turned away to respond to something his trainer, Beau, was saying, but not before he caught the knowing smile on her lips.

Cambree unpacked her bag quickly, staring in awe at the gorgeous little cabin she'd be staying in for a week. She was here. She had truly made it, and if memory served her correctly, she'd also met Emmett Hawk a few minutes before and hadn't allowed her too-honest tongue to make a complete fool out of herself. She pinched herself and squealed at the same time. Emmett Hawk. The boys in her sixth-grade class were going to be so jealous. Was it too quick to ask for a selfie with him? Many of her students followed her on Instagram and had helped raise the money to get her to this camp in preparation for her summer of Warrior races.

She stashed her suitcase in the closet and looked around one more time at the pristine cabin and its luxurious features: the decorative woodwork, the distressed wood floors, the plush rugs, the massive king-sized bed—it was softer than a baby's butt; she'd jumped on it to test it—the leather couches in a nook by the picture window that faced the forest, and the glass shower and huge jetted tub in the bathroom, all done in granite, of course. Growing up in Breckenridge, Colorado, she'd helped her mama clean some beautiful homes, but of course she'd never stayed in a five-star resort like this. At twenty thousand for the week, she supposed the accommodations had to be plush.

But she wouldn't have cared if they were sleeping under the stars. Emmett Hawk was going to train her, and she was going to absolutely rock the rest of her races this summer. She wanted number one badly, mostly to prove to herself she could do it and that Nolan wasn't right that she was trailer trash and would never amount to anything. Luckily her sport wasn't popular enough that she had to do interviews or anything terrifying like that.

She hurried to freshen up, putting on an extra layer of clinical-strength antiperspirant. The advertisers claimed it was stink-proof, so she wouldn't reek if by some miracle she got to train with Emmett Hawk. She didn't want to miss out on one minute of this experience. It'd taken a lot of saving, months of being tighter financially than an eighty-year-old hoarder, to get here. Her students had organized fundraisers for her all on their own, and that had been so appreciated and adorable. She just knew this elite fitness camp was going to make the difference in her success this summer, and as the most gargantuan bonus known to woman, she got to be around Emmett Hawk.

The promotional info claimed Emmett would be involved in the actual training of the participants. Besides being one of the top wide receivers in the nation, he also had a master's degree in exercise physiology. Yes, she'd Googled him. Weekly. He and his brothers were all plastered everywhere online. The mighty Hawk brothers. They were all undeniably handsome, buff, poised, and accomplished. She couldn't blame the media for hanging on every word they said, but she did hate how it picked apart every woman they dated. At least she wouldn't be exposed to that while she enjoyed being starstruck by Emmett this week.

This camp hadn't been easy to get into; there had been essays and recommendations required, and attendance was capped at only twenty people. She wondered when the rest of the participants would show up. She liked everyone she'd met on the shuttle ride from the airport, except Troy; he was a little stalkerish creepy with his penetrating looks. She connected most with Gunner, who was so cute with his dimples and curly hair. Nana Lucy was a crackup, though Cambree wasn't sure why she was so hard on Britney. The older lady looked fit, but Cambree wondered how she'd gotten into the camp that was supposed to be for athletes.

Walking out the cabin door, she stopped and stared, blinking against the brightness of Emmett Hawk's glory. He stood a mere twenty feet away, talking to one of the other male trainers. Dressed in a fitted neoprene shirt and cotton shorts, Emmett was as handsome and fit as any man had a right to be, maybe more. His dark hair was short and his tanned skin was smooth.

He had one of those Hollywood gorgeous faces, complete with the shortly trimmed facial hair. Yummy.

Emmett glanced her direction and their eyes caught and held. His dark gaze was welcoming, and she was drawn in like a tractor beam. She was pretty sure she walked toward him and he walked toward her, but she couldn't remember her limbs actually being put in motion. Then he stood before her, or rather above her. She was a respectable five-seven, but he dwarfed her. His stats said six-five and two-forty, and the muscles displayed by that tight shirt backed those stats up and then some.

"Cambree." The way he said her name, drawling out the soft A and making *bree* its own beautiful sigh from his lips, made her think her parents had been brilliant to choose it. His voice was all deep and husky, and his lips couldn't be hidden by that perfect facial hair—they were too full and delicious-looking. He cleared his throat and said, "Did you get settled in?"

"Oh my, yes. It's so beautiful here!" The words burst out too exuberantly, and she felt like a sixteen-year-old.

"Glad you like it." His eyes trailed over her casual dress. "Are you comfortable working out in that?"

Cambree's face flared. She should've changed into workout gear. "Wow, didn't know the bossy man was already putting me to work."

He grinned. "Don't worry. I'll go easy on you."

"You'd better not. I paid heaps of hard-earned money so you could kick my tush into shape." Now her face warmed further at her mention of how expensive this camp was.

Emmett didn't seem bothered by her comment at all. Score another point for the superstar. "You look like you're already in fabulous shape."

Cambree acknowledged the compliment with a chin nod.

"But it's your lucky job to take my body to the next level so I can be number one this year."

"Challenge accepted." He grinned.

Britney strode up to Emmett and placed her hand on his arm, interrupting their conversation. Cambree would've liked to chitchat with the superstar longer, but she understood everyone wanted his attention and she worried that she'd say something offensive to him. Britney had all the composure and confidence you'd expect from a supermodel. Cambree was sure it wouldn't be hard for any man to give her attention. Cambree saw a lot of different workout apparel worn at Warrior races, but she didn't know they made shorts as short as Britney wore them. Her cheeks were literally hanging out.

"You think you can take *my* body to the next level?" Britney purred.

Cambree's face reddened again. When she'd asked Emmett to take her to the next level, she'd meant her fitness, not her shape or any other ... things to do with her body. She hoped it hadn't sounded like an innuendo. Yikes. She was so out of her league socially. She was a solo Warrior racer, and that's the way she trained as well. These people probably weren't going to interact like her sixth graders, who thought she was funny when she put her foot in her mouth.

"Maybe he can give her a swift kick where her shorts should be," Nana Lucy said in Cambree's ear.

Cambree laughed, almost more from surprise than amusement, and instantly felt bad as Britney glared over at them, not releasing her hold on Emmett.

Emmett clapped his hands together, gently dislodging Britney's arm, and said, "Looks like everybody's here and ready to get started."

Cambree hadn't noticed Troy and Gunner. She looked over her right shoulder. Gunner waved, friendly and cute as ever. Troy leered at her and ran his tongue over his lips. Cambree flipped back around. Competing in a co-ed sport, she'd had more than her share of men hitting on her. Sometimes it was a compliment, and sometimes it was just terrifying.

She looked back at Emmett and noticed his jaw tightening as he glared at Troy. Could it be possible Emmett Hawk was interested in her? No. That was crazy thinking. He was a billionaire hunk with hundreds of times more women pursuing him than the zeros in his net worth. Cambree was nowhere on the radar of a Hawk brother. She was born to a single mom who had absolutely no social graces. Her mom made Cambree's errant tongue sound like a church choir.

No, Cambree could never date someone like Emmett Hawk. He was probably annoyed with Troy because he didn't want any romances going on this week when they should be focusing on transforming their bodies and learning how to push their fitness to the next level.

"It's a small group this round," Emmett continued. "Crazily enough, the other fifteen participants dropped out for one reason or another."

Cambree wondered how strong of a reason she would need to back out of this dream opportunity. Besides a death in the family, she really couldn't think of anything. Emmett seemed a little embarrassed the others had dropped out. Surely he didn't think it was a reflection on him? Anyone with a brain between their ears would want to be near him.

"So we'll keep it pretty informal. Let's go around and introduce ourselves and what we hope to achieve this week." He smiled. "I'll start. I'm Emmett Hawk."

"We all know who *you* are." Britney smiled at him, and Cambree could see why she was such a fabulous model. Any woman would want to imitate her sultry yet somehow innocent look, and any man would buy anything Britney was selling.

"If I have to listen to her say one more word, I'm going to vomit," Lucy said.

Cambree shushed her with a finger to her lips. She thought the older lady's snark was funny, but Cambree tried never to put someone in a cage simply because they were beautiful or famous, no matter that her ex-fiancé, Nolan, had explained in great detail that Cambree would never be on their level. She didn't understand the social elite world, but was it their fault they were born to money and prestige any more than it was Cambree's fault she was born in a trailer park? Britney probably had lots of depth to her; she just wasn't ... showing it as well as she was showing her cleavage up front and in the behind.

"So I guess you all know I'm a wide receiver for the Titans?" Emmett smirked, and Cambree thought he was absolutely exquisite. Confident, but not cocky.

"Rookie of the year. Highest-paid rookie ever," Gunner called out. "Yeah, we know all about you and are struggling with the hero worship, man." He gave a thumbs-up.

Cambree was glad Gunner was here. He was friendly, and everything he said was positive. She caught a glance of Troy's sneer. Maybe he didn't appreciate Gunner's cheerleader style.

Lucy and Britney both clapped and said, "Go Titans!" at the same time. Britney giggled adorably. Lucy shook her head. "Ay bendito, now I'm a groupie."

Emmett chuckled. "So you've probably also heard that I ripped out every ligament in my knee at the all-star event, and

…" He looked down. "I'm not gonna lie, the recovery has been rough, but I'll get back."

Silence blanketed the group, and Cambree's heart went out to Emmett. She could only imagine how hard he'd worked to be where he was, and to be injured, to have to start all over? That was brutal.

"Ah, man, sorry to hear it," Gunner said. "But if anyone can get back, it'll be you. You're a Hawk, right?"

Everyone murmured their agreement.

"Thanks." Emmett moved on quickly. "So I started this camp because I want to give back, and I couldn't stand the thought of just sitting around dealing with physical therapists."

They all laughed.

"This is my fourth week of the Titans fitness camp and my first with adults. The first two weeks were sixteen- to eighteen-year-olds. Last week was college athletes. I guess the college group can be considered adults."

"Naw, we don't want to grow up," Gunner said.

Cambree couldn't imagine how Gunner could ever grow up. He reminded her of the carefree attitude of her eighteen-year-old brother, who their mother worried would amount to nothing but dating the town's rodeo queen. He had a construction job, though, so Cambree tried to remind her mom of that.

"This week," Emmett said, "I wanted to focus on adult athletes and on adults who simply want to increase their fitness level and be healthier."

"Old farts like me," Lucy said.

"I'd never say that, ma'am." Emmett grinned, the teasing lilt to his voice and his smile were both irresistible.

"I really just signed up to have him grin at me like that," Lucy muttered so only Cambree could hear. Cambree laughed softly and completely agreed. That smile aimed her direction was more than worth the twenty-thousand-dollar price tag. She sobered up quickly. No, she had to focus and excel this week, not just be smitten by Emmett Hawk's smile, though any woman would struggle to not be smitten.

"It's crazy that we had so many dropouts this week. The past camps had none, except for one little guy who broke his arm skateboarding the day before he came, but I think for each of you this will be an amazing opportunity." He gestured to the trainers standing around him. "You'll each get individual training most of the week. We'll still do some things in groups, but mostly we'll work one-on-one so we can maximize your time here and focus on exactly what you want to achieve." He spread his hands. "So it's your turn. Tell us who you are and what you're here to accomplish." He inclined his chin to Britney, who was still standing so close to him that the blond trainer had been displaced from his spot. The guy seemed to be struggling to keep his eyes off of Britney's backside.

"Hi, I'm Britney." She smiled that sweet smile of hers. "You probably all recognize me."

Lucy muttered, "Maybe if you'd take all your clothes off we could recognize you better."

Britney's smile drooped.

"Hush that tongue," Cambree said. "There's no call to be low-down mean."

Lucy looked surprised at the retort. Cambree wondered if she'd gone too far, but she didn't like bullies in any form. The entire group stared at her, but it was Emmett's warm gaze that made her feel like she'd done all right standing up for Britney.

The silence seemed to lengthen.

"So your goals are?" Emmett prompted Britney.

"I'm here to have you make my body even more perfect." Britney looked worshipfully at Emmett. "And I loved the idea of a fitness retreat. Who doesn't love to be pampered? Right, girls?" She grinned broadly at Cambree as if they were close friends.

Cambree forced a smile because she wanted to be friends with everyone at the camp, but she had never been pampered a day in her life, so she didn't really know how to commiserate. As the oldest of six children with a single mom who worked hard cleaning wealthy people's homes to make ends meet, Cambree couldn't remember a day, besides Sundays, she hadn't either babysat and kept things in line at home, or helped her mom at a cleaning job. Her family had been super proud when she'd graduated from CSU and gotten a teaching job. She was the first one to have a college degree of any of her relations.

"You can rub my bunions later," Lucy joked.

Everyone laughed, and Cambree hoped any hard feelings between Britney and Lucy would be gone.

Britney wrinkled her delicate nose. "I'm sure they have people who do that."

"We do, actually," Emmett interjected. "After you work hard every day, we have a full spa where you will get massages, pedicures, facials, whatever you want."

"Yes!" Lucy pumped her fist in the air. "Now if I can just get through the 'work hard' part."

Emmett smiled. "What's your story, Nana Lucy?"

"Just wanting to perfect my body so I'm ready when *Sports Illustrated* calls me up." She winked at Britney, but it wasn't a friendly wink, too mocking.

The female trainer, Tracy, laughed. Emmett gave the woman a quick look, then turned back to Lucy, folding his impressive arms across his even more impressive chest. "I want the truth now. We're going to get close this week, and I want us cheering each other on, not tearing down. I just shared my biggest fear with you: not being able to play ... the first few games of this season. Please drop the snark and tell us why you're here."

"Sorry, Britney." Lucy actually sounded repentant, and Britney gave her a nod of acknowledgment. "Snark is my only defense." She sighed and then pushed out, "My husband of thirty-one years cheated on me with a twenty-two-year-old swimsuit model."

Britney's eyes widened and she took a step back, planting her foot on one of the tall male trainers. He steadied her and smiled.

"I've always worked hard to take care of myself, stay attractive for my husband." She shook her head. "I came this week to find me again, see if I had any toughness and grit left in me that that jerkbait Tim didn't steal when he busted my illusions of a happy marriage and loving each other forever."

Silence fell on the group. No wonder Lucy was such a smart aleck. It was to protect her battered heart. Cambree turned and wrapped the woman up in a hug. "You look super tough to me," she said.

Lucy squeezed her back. "Thanks." She straightened her shoulders and Cambree let her go. "It was either this or plastic surgery. This seemed less painful." She grinned and was back to her playful self.

Cambree appreciated the insight into the older lady, and it definitely made sense why she struggled with Britney. Cambree wondered if Britney didn't have a sad story she wasn't sharing. Everybody had been through hard things, right?

"And you?" Lucy stared at Cambree.

Cambree smiled at everyone in the group, anxious to get to know the trainers as well as the participants. "I'm a sixth-grade teacher and a Warrior racer. I made it into the elite category last year, but crashed and burned hard on my pursuit of number one." She took a breath and continued, encouraged by Emmett's friendly smile and that she hadn't said anything too honest or embarrassing yet. "My students helped me raise the fat wad of cash to get here." Britney's eyebrows rose at that, and Cambree rushed on to finish. "With Emmett Hawk training me, I'm going to hit number one at the Breckenridge race, which is in my hometown. I'll be a hometown hero!"

She punched a fist in the air, and then felt kind of stupid until Gunner whooped and started clapping. Lucy and Britney joined him, and then the trainers and Emmett did as well. The only one who didn't cheer was Troy. He simply looked at her like she was a prime rib dinner.

When the cheering died down, Emmett said, "Good for you, Cambree. I'm excited to work with you." The moment went sticky and slow between them as their eyes met. Was this for real? Was Emmett Hawk really staring into her eyes? Score one for Cambree.

Lucy broke the interaction with a low whistle. "I haven't seen that much sparks and fire since the chemistry lab at Texas A&M exploded."

"Much more fun than a fire." Cambree blushed and looked away when everyone's eyebrows rose.

"Gunner?" Emmett said in a gruff voice.

"You know my story, man: hoping to make the NFL so I need to rock my senior year at Florida State."

"You've come to the right place. We know football." Emmett grinned. "Jacob played for Auburn and Beau for Alabama. Don't worry, they try to be civil to each other."

"Roll Tide," said the trainer near Britney. One of the other trainers said something about a war eagle.

"What about you, Troy?" asked Emmett.

"Same as Gunner," he grunted.

"All right." Emmett nodded around the group. "Happy to have you all here. I for one am stoked that our numbers are so small. We can personalize each of your programs, and even though a week isn't a lot of time, it's enough to push you to the next level as well as teach you how to push yourself and help you establish successful habits." He gestured behind him. "Tracy?"

The pretty brunette smiled. "I specialize in fitness competitions and working with models and actresses, so Britney and I will have a lot of one-on-one time."

Britney smiled but didn't look thrilled. She kept staring at Emmett, but he didn't focus on her at all.

The dark-haired Jacob stepped forward. "Like Emmett said, Beau and I—" Beau simply raised his hand. "—both played college ball, so we'll be working closely with Gunner and Troy."

Gunner gave them the hang-loose sign. Troy looked like he wanted to flash them a different gesture, but simply clenched his arms tighter across his broad chest.

Mark smiled. He had a California surfer look with blue eyes and longish blond hair. "And I am the expert at making the ex-husband wish he had never dumped such a beautiful lady." He winked at Lucy.

"Oh yeah, man!" Lucy punched both fists in the air. "We'll make him try to crawl back and then kick him square in the butt. I love you, Mark!"

Mark and everyone else laughed. Lucy was so funny that everyone could tease with her and it wouldn't ever go to an inappropriate place—at least, Cambree hoped not.

"Well, no time like the present," Emmett said. "Go get your workout gear on and we'll go on a short run, then have lunch and a tour of the facility before we pair off and really get working." His eyes gleamed, and Cambree could see he loved what he did.

As she walked away to her small cabin, she wondered if she was dreaming or if she was about to get paired off with Emmett Hawk. All the other trainers had basically claimed their trainees, but nobody had claimed her, and Emmett hadn't claimed anyone. She clasped her palms together and prayed she'd done enough right in this world to be able to have one-on-one time with the handsomest of the famously perfect Hawk brothers.

CHAPTER TWO

Emmett wanted to start the one-on-one training with Cambree immediately, but he worried he'd been too transparent during introductions. Lucy had called them out in front of the entire group, and he didn't want anyone thinking he was playing favorites. Yet all of his trainers had played into his scheming perfectly, each claiming one of the other participants. Emmett wouldn't mind doing some one-on-one with Troy or Gunner, but he wasn't getting anywhere near Britney. He and his brothers got plenty of media exposure without having someone like Britney clinging to them. She was beautiful but not his type at all. He knew she loved to splay her body and her boyfriends all over the media. He had no desire to get caught in that trap.

His thoughts swung back around to Cambree easily, like a pendulum that wanted to settle on her beautiful face. The upside of everyone at the camp knowing he was attracted to Cambree was that maybe Britney would back off.

Cambree walked out of her cabin, and his heart pumped

quicker. Now *that* was appealing. Her dark hair was pulled up in a ponytail that trailed down her back with riotous curls. Her smooth neck was revealed in a V-neck T-shirt, but it wasn't low enough to show any kind of cleavage. Her toned legs were displayed perfectly by fitted black athletic shorts, but they covered her to mid-thigh and neither she nor Emmett would be uncomfortable if she bent over or squatted.

She caught his gaze and smiled, lifting a hand. "What's the plan, bossy man?" she asked.

He couldn't resist crossing the open area, shaded with pine trees, to meet her. He liked the way she talked. "You'll think I'm bossy after a week."

"I think you're bossy already." She gave him a sassy smile and he ate it right up.

"Ready for a short run? Running's easy for you, right?"

"Don't let it out, but I'd rather eat Spam than run. It's my least favorite part of Warrior." She put a little Western inflection on "Spam" and wrinkled her nose adorably, and Emmett wondered if he'd ever said or even thought the word adorable before. He also wondered if she'd really eaten Spam. He'd heard of the nasty fake meat, but the worst meat he'd ever tried was some greasy taco place his college buddies had dragged him to.

"We'll make you so strong the running will be easy."

"Big talker. Can you make the burpees easy too?"

"Just don't get penalties and you won't need to do them."

She laughed. "Easier said than done. What do they do to your tough self when you screw up at football practice?"

Emmett kind of hated thinking about practice. What would he do when the regular season started and he wasn't practicing or playing? He'd thought he could keep the fitness camps going year round for adults and mostly focus on the youth in the summer, but if this week's fail was any indication, maybe adults weren't willing to take a week off and pay a premium price to become more fit.

He pushed all of that away and flirted with Cambree, a little shocked she'd said "screw up." Language was much worse than that on the field, but off the field the people he was around were too civilized to talk like that. Taking a step closer, he said, "I never make a mistake, so I don't know."

She placed a hand on his chest. He wasn't sure if it was to make him keep his distance or because she wanted to touch him. Fire raced through him at her simple touch. "Ha," she muttered, and he could see how fast her breath was coming. He really liked that he affected her. "Everybody messes up sometimes."

"Not me. Near perfect. Ask my mom."

She removed her hand, which he hated, and gave him a brilliant smile, which he loved. "Those mamas. Can't trust their biased opinions."

"Did your mom make you feel like you were the best thing in the world too?" he asked.

Cambree nodded. "My mama would put a professional cheerleader to shame."

He grinned, commiserating. His parents could've bought any box in the Titans' stadium, but his mom insisted on front-row seats so her boy could see how proud she was. Man, he was going to miss seeing them up in the stands. "My mom asked me once why I didn't brag about myself. I told her she bragged enough for the both of us."

Cambree laughed. "Well, I hate to admit this and swell your head even more, but she has a lot to brag about."

He liked her, and it appeared she liked him too. She was very different from any woman he'd been around. It was refreshing and intriguing.

"We hate to interrupt, but I think this is a fitness camp, not Flirtation 101." Lucy was grinning at the two of them.

Emmett returned her smile and wondered how everyone else had snuck up on them. Cambree was an expert at capturing all of his attention. "Short run through the property to warm up," he said. He took off at a fast jog to let everyone warm up, and felt a surge of happiness when Cambree stayed by his side.

The group stayed in a pretty tight pack for the first couple of miles, nobody saying much besides Britney trying to flirt with Emmett a little bit. Then Lucy smarted off. "What do you consider a *long* run?"

"Twenty miles or more," Emmett threw back at her.

"Somebody shoot me now," Lucy groaned. "Or maybe I'll just die of the heat."

Emmett laughed. It was a June day in Texas, probably high nineties, and he had sweat dripping down his back. The trail they were running along was shady and by the lake, so it tempered the heat to manageable.

Troy, Britney, Lucy, Tracy, and Mark dropped back a little bit. Gunner was chatting with Beau and Jacob about football. Cambree had claimed she didn't like to run, but she was keeping pace easily. Emmett's knee was throbbing, but he ignored it. Even though the doctors claimed he couldn't injure the manufactured parts, he would probably always have pain. The injury had been four months ago and at least he didn't have to wear the brace anymore.

"How long are we running?" Cambree asked as they jogged along the path next to the oblong lake. They had rowboats out there that were only occasionally used. Sometimes one of the trainers would have a participant swim in the lake, but it was easier to use the Olympic-size pool next to the lodge.

"It's about a six-mile loop."

"Easy money." Cambree smiled at him.

"For you. I knew you were a good runner."

"Liar. You'd never heard my lowly name before today."

"Not true. I researched all of the participants so I could line them up with the right trainer, and I was able to watch you in some of your races. I was impressed. You're even pre— ... more impressive in person." He risked a glance at her, and her angelic face was so open and trusting. She didn't act like she'd even noticed his slip.

"You're not too shabby yourself," Cambree said. "I guess with your family you can't help but be a superstar."

"True." His mom thought her boys could do no wrong, but his dad expected his sons to shine and had never tolerated anything but working toward perfection. "What do you know about my family?"

She shrugged. "Just that the Hawk brothers are all hardworking, individual, successful, and hand— ... impressive."

He chuckled. She had noticed his slip. "Are you okay with me admitting that you're beautiful?"

Cambree's eyes widened and her cheeks got redder than the run was making them. "If you're okay with me admitting that you're handsome."

He smiled. "I guess I'm okay with that."

"With a face like yours, you're probably sick of hearing it."

He shrugged, feeling his face flush. "My mom never got tired of telling me how handsome I was, but I thought it was only her who believed it, until I started playing in the NFL and all these articles started being printed about 'hottest football player' and all that crap."

"Oh, poor baby. Must've been hard on you."

He laughed and shook his head. "Time to change the subject. Tell me about your family."

They had made it to the end of the lake, and the path curved. Emmett noticed he and Cambree had a decent lead on the rest of the crew. He was surprised Troy hadn't tried to run faster to prove how tough he was, but Troy was actually smiling at the back and talking to Britney, so that was a pleasant surprise. Maybe Britney would stay away from Emmett, and even more importantly, Troy would stay away from Cambree. Emmett hated the lewd looks he'd seen Troy give Cambree already.

"Well, we're nobody like the famous Hawk family." Her voice was cautious and almost scared.

"We're just normal people, Cambree," he said.

Her eyebrows rose, but she didn't comment.

"Do you have siblings?" He wanted to draw her out, and he understood that his family would be intimidating if you didn't know them.

She nodded. "I'm the oldest of six. Two sisters and three brothers. My youngest brother, Luke, is a huge fan of yours, by the way. Hero worship doesn't begin to describe the obsession."

"Ah, I like him already." Though it made him uncomfortable to have anybody worshipping him. He was a quitter and it rubbed him wrong. His brother, Creed, was a Navy SEAL, and he was going to be disappointed when he found out Emmett couldn't work his way back. "Who's closest to you?"

"My sister Jasmine. She didn't get a scholarship like I did for college, so she went to beauty school. She's a major sweetie and just got engaged to her high school sweetheart. He has a machine shop and is ultra-successful. We're all so proud. Well ..."

Emmett liked to listen to her talk. It was intriguing and real. Cambree was a person he'd notice in a crowd, and not just because of her beauty. The pause stretched on, and Emmett looked at her and prompted, "Well?"

"Successful for our hometown. Nothing compared to the Hawk Dynasty." She gestured to him.

"Don't do that," Emmett said, though he loved how honest she was. He didn't know anybody who spoke so candidly to him besides his brothers, mom, and coaches. "Working hard and earning your way is a huge success."

"Gracias." She bowed kind of mockingly at him.

They jogged in silence for a while, heading back toward the lodge and cabins.

"I'm sorry," she said. "Sometimes I make things awkward." Emmett tried to protest, but she continued, "You're this icon and your family are, like, the princes of America. It's as foreign to me as a famous opera singer being from Arkansas."

Emmett had to laugh at her last line, but he didn't like the division between them and the way she perceived his family. It shouldn't matter. He hardly knew her, and a romance with a fitness camp attendee wasn't part of the plan, but he really, really liked her. "I promise we're normal. My brothers and I wrestled like monkeys, and our mom baked us cookies and scolded us, and our dad was always there to give us 'the talk' about living up to our potential and making the Hawks look good. He did attend all of our sporting events."

"Looking perfect doesn't sound fun."

"No," he agreed.

They were silent for a few beats. Then she said, "Tell me

about your brothers."

He sensed she already knew all about them, but he pretended they were normal and not on the paparazzi radar at all times. "Callum's the oldest. He runs Dad's businesses and takes himself much too seriously. We tease him he should just sew his phone to his ear."

She laughed. "Maybe you should get him a Bluetooth for Christmas."

"He claims they don't look professional. I think he likes people seeing him strutting around on his phone. All important-looking."

"You don't like Callum?" She looked askance at him.

Emmett shrugged. "We're not close, but he's a good guy. You'll have to meet him to understand."

Her eyebrows rose, and Emmett realized what he'd insinuated. He hardly knew her, and he'd just implied she was going to meet his family. He didn't even take the women he dated home to meet his mom.

He rushed on. "Creed is next. He's a Navy SEAL." Pride crept into his voice, and he didn't try to hide it. Creed was a superhero to him, and his success had nothing to do with money or social status and everything to do with working his tail off to be the best.

"That's amazing. Where is he stationed?"

"Syria right now. He's got a mission coming up that he's worried about. I mean, he never would say that, but I can hear it, you know?"

She nodded. "My daddy was a policeman, killed in a shootout with some drug dealers." Her eyes widened after she spoke, and she upped her pace.

"I'm so sorry," Emmett said.

"No. I shouldn't have said that. Your brother won't get killed. I'm sorry."

"I'm sorry about your dad."

She shook her head, and Emmett was amazed they'd gotten to this depth of conversation, but running with somebody did that—you opened up and shared all.

"And your last brother?" she asked.

She obviously wanted to move on, and he did too. Thinking about Creed getting killed made his neck tighten and emotion rise to the surface. He was closest to Creed and loved his confidence and the way he teased. Emmett couldn't stand the thought of losing him, but they all knew Creed's life was anything but safe. It terrified his parents, yet they were both very proud of Creed.

"Bridger." He couldn't help but smile. "He's the youngest and he's a ... punk."

"Excuse me?" Cambree let out a surprised laugh. "I'm the one who says things too bluntly."

Emmett chuckled. "You're right, I shouldn't say that about my brother. He's hilarious and just ... sucks the marrow out of life. He can make a joke out of anything and everything, and it makes my dad and Callum about crazy." He kept talking, partially because he loved talking about Bridger, but mostly because focusing on Bridger took away the darkness of Creed being in constant danger and Cambree sharing that her dad had died. He hated that she'd gone through that. He wanted to know how old she'd been when he was killed and how her mom had dealt and was dealing with being a single mom, and if any of her siblings were struggling, but he tried to keep things light and focus on Bridger. "Have you ever seen that show *Point Break*?"

"I saw the new one and the old one."

"So Bridger is like one of those guys. Life's all about the next thrill, and he and his friends take nothing seriously."

"I actually saw him at the world surfing finales on TV, and he is wicked awesome," she gushed. He must've pulled a face, because she backtracked. "I mean, if he isn't your brother, it's cool what he does. They call him an extreme athlete, right?"

"Yeah. Lately he's been focusing on wakeboarding and getting ready for the X Games. My mom is actually thrilled with this venture, because wakeboarding is safer than heli-skiing, cave diving, big wave surfing, ice climbing, or wingsuit flying." They were almost back to the main lodge and open grassy area now. Emmett had to blame it on the comfortable running pace and pleasant company that he kept sharing so much about his family, but the beautiful, candid lady at his side was easy to talk to. "My mom says it's hard enough Creed puts his life on the line for his country. Bridger puts his life on the line for an adrenaline rush."

"Ooh. I bet that pisses her right off." Cambree blew out a breath. "I hate that for her, and I don't even know either of them."

Had she really said the word "pisses"? Emmett had to fight not to laugh. She was definitely not his usual date. Not that he was dating her. Cambree was looking at him, so he continued, "It is tough on her, but if you spent five minutes with Bridger, you just can't help but like the kid. He's kind of like Gunner."

Cambree smiled. "Gunner's a stud muffin."

And just like that, Emmett's gut tightened with jealousy. He shook it off, and they slowed to a walk as they approached the manicured lawn next to the main lodge. The group filtered in next to them and Emmett turned to Tracy. "Why don't you lead us in a cooldown, then we'll eat lunch, do a tour of the facility, and do individual sessions after that?"

"Sounds great." Tracy started into some yoga stretches, which were even more effective with their muscles warm from the run. Emmett found his gaze straying to Cambree time and again. He'd loved chatting with her on the run. He'd opened up more than he'd thought possible in such a short time.

His knee ached as they bent into a squat, and he was reminded of the lie he was telling the world right now, pretending to be getting ready for the season when in reality he was a washout. Should he tell Cambree the truth? He shook his head. His agent and his dad's media advisors were insistent nobody knew until Emmett made the announcement that he'd be focusing on his fitness camps and stepping down from the Titans. It had to look like his choice and not dictated by his knee or his coaches, or the whole camp idea would just look like a desperate washed-out player trying to hold on to something he'd lost. Only Emmett and those few people would know the truth. If only there was another path for him that led back to football.

CHAPTER THREE

Cambree was even more impressed with the camp after they ate a buffet-style lunch that was delicious, fresh, and had more variety than her sixth-grade girls had mood swings. Then they took the tour of the facility, and she had to clench her jaw to keep it from dropping. She caught Emmett watching her for a reaction a few times. He really seemed to give a flip what she thought, but she wondered if her reaction just made her look like even more of a hick. They came from different worlds. Polar opposite worlds. She'd thought her ex-fiancé was high-society, but he was nothing compared to Emmett. The only time she could say she and Emmett truly related was her having lost her dad and his fear of losing his brother. Still, it had been rocking to chat while they ran. Nothing like a run to get somebody to spill their crap.

They each paired off and started training for their specific events. Cambree had been hoping Emmett would be her trainer, and when he motioned to her and they walked together into the open gym area, an area he'd told them they'd added at the first of the summer for the camps, she finally dared ask, "So does this mean you're the dopest trainer for a Warrior racer?"

"Yes, ma'am." He winked, and her heart seemed to stutter before restarting. "Maybe not the best in the world, but the best at this camp."

"You'd better be the rocking best boy. I'm counting on you to make me flex on everybody else. Number one or nothing, baby."

"You're already number one in my book." He gave her a goofy smile.

"That was cheesy, Hawk."

"I like you calling me Hawk." He took a small step closer, but it was enough she could smell warm and musky cologne and she could see the sparkle in his dark eyes. The gym around them disappeared, and she couldn't remember a single goal besides staying close to this splendid man.

"And they're at it again." Lucy's dry voice came from behind them. "You two going to actually work out this week, or is the pitter-patter of your hearts enough of a workout?"

Emmett chuckled and took a step back. "You focus on your own exercise, Nana Lucy, and stop worrying about us."

She laughed and took the weighted bar Mark handed her, then followed his instructions to drop into some deep walking lunges across the gym floor.

Emmett led Cambree through a quick warm-up of squats, inchworms, planks, and toy soldiers, then said, "Let's start with burpees."

Cambree planted her hands on her hips. "You said I wouldn't have any penalties, so no burpees."

"Rule number one: you do *exactly* what I say." Emmett stepped closer, and suddenly she was surrounded by his musky smell, his strength, the sheer manliness of him. It wasn't intimidating—it was inspiring.

"I knew you were a bossy man."

He lifted an eyebrow and commanded, "Burpees."

Cambree groaned but complied.

Emmett counted for her. "9 ... 10 ... 11 ... No, no, no! You didn't touch your chest to the ground."

Cambree jumped up and glared at him. "You'd better back up a step, sucker."

He chuckled. "You'd better get it right. Watch and learn." He dropped into a squat, quickly kicked his legs out behind him, did a perfect push-up, then jumped his legs back in and leapt toward the air. "I want you jumping higher too. Now go."

Cambree folded her arms and glared at him. "The rules clearly state I only have to clear my feet off the ground. I'm not wasting precious energy jumping around like a bunny rabbit." Her pride stung from him saying she didn't touch her chest to the ground.

Emmett stepped closer, and the intense look on his handsome face was a little intimidating this time. He wasn't going to let her get away with anything. "I am training you to be the best and the toughest, and when you're in an actual competition and the burpees feel easy, you can thank me then." He arched an eyebrow and dared her to question him, which she wasn't about to do. "Now go!"

Cambree rolled her eyes but complied, dropping down into a burpee, exaggerating hitting her chest on the floor, then leaping into a squat position and using her powerful quad muscles to fly as high as she could jump.

"Yes! That's my girl. Keep going."

Cambree felt warmth rush through her. *His girl.* She wasn't, not even close, but she loved the way he'd said that. Those three words gave her a burst of energy, and she pumped out thirty burpees without complaint, though her thighs were burning, before he yelled, "Now sprint!"

Cambree took off running across the gym, passing Lucy and Mark. Lucy was still doing walking lunges.

"Go, Cambree!" Lucy hollered. "Sheesh, she's fast."

"Yeah," Mark agreed.

Their cheering helped also, and she upped her speed.

"Ten lengths of the gym," Emmett called.

Cambree was feeling the burpees and the sprinting by her sixth length. She realized she should not have eaten quite so much at the delectable lunch spread. It wasn't going to taste nearly as good coming back up.

Emmett was suddenly by her side, and watching him run was a glorious thing. He was so long and well-built that he seemed to glide over the polished floor. "Come on, sweetie, you got this," he encouraged her as they sprinted together.

When she hit the wall at ten, she gasped for air and put her hands on her knees.

"Nice!" Emmett said. "Now army crawl four lengths of the gym."

Cambree groaned but complied. She couldn't help but wonder if he called all the girls he trained "my girl" and "sweetie," but it definitely helped to motivated her. She was pretty sure she rubbed all the skin off her forearms by the time she finished the fourth length of army crawl, but she was used to that with the barbed wire crawl being a staple of most of her events, and that obstacle was through dirt, rocks, and sometimes muddy water.

"Thirty burpees," Emmett said.

"What? I didn't mess up."

Emmett simply raised an eyebrow at her. "Your race clock is ticking."

"Jerk," she muttered, but she started the burpees.

"Jump higher!" Emmett hollered.

She finally reached thirty and could hardly breathe. Her legs were quivering.

"Sprint," Emmett commanded.

Cambree took off. Part of her was hating her trainer, but another part of her was loving Emmett, loving this. It was why she'd raised the money and traveled to Texas: to be pushed harder than she could push herself. Even though it was excruciating and painful, it felt great, in a twisted psycho sort of way.

On the eighth length, Emmett joined her again. She wondered how his knee was holding up, but she had no oxygen to ask.

"You got this. I love your speed," Emmett said.

Cambree took that as a huge compliment from the man who could do the forty-yard dash in barely over four seconds. They raced to the end of the gym, and Cambree slammed into the padded wall again.

"Rope climb," Emmett said, a little out of breath himself, gesturing toward the corner of the gym.

Cambree loved this obstacle. She hurried to the rope and grasped it, scurrying up to the top, then sliding down.

"That was impressive. Thirty burpees."

Cambree didn't even groan, just complied. She'd never have this many burpees in an actual event, but if she kept this up, she'd be quicker than anybody at them.

As she finished the last burpee, Emmett gestured to the rope. "Climb it again."

"Give me something hard, bossy man," she threw at him.

He looked surprised for half a second. Then he laughed. "You got this, sweetheart."

Cambree didn't know if she should tell him the terms of endearment were a huge motivator for her, or if she should just keep her mouth shut. It was possible he didn't realize he was using them, and she definitely didn't want him to stop. She climbed quickly up the rope and slid down. Five feet from the ground she let go, but instead of catching her, her exhausted legs gave out. She hit the gym floor hard.

Emmett was right there. He lifted her up, and Cambree should've cared that she probably reeked of sweat, but it was just too nice to be in his muscular arms. Sheesh, he smelled good and he felt good and she was so exhausted she wanted to lie against his chest and fall asleep. Well, there might not be any sleeping if she stayed in these arms. Too invigorating.

"You okay, sweetheart?" His dark eyes were concerned, but they also burned with a "stay in these buff arms of mine" smolder.

"Fabulous." She forced herself to pull back, though it was tougher than anything he'd thrown at her today. "What's next?"

Emmett blinked and then whooped. "That's my girl! You're a beast."

Cambree knew being called a beast was a compliment in her brothers' lingo, but she'd assumed a high-society guy like Emmett wouldn't use the word. Football must've softened him up, and the way Emmett's dark eyes were sparkling at her made her feel amazing and like she was his girl. It was so different from the way her ex, Nolan, had made her feel when he abruptly dumped her, that she wanted to savor it.

There was no time for sappy thinking like that. Emmett

grabbed a bucket and lifted it easily, making Cambree grit her teeth. He put the eighty-pound bucket in her hands and said, "As you pointed out, we don't have any mountains in Texas, so we'll have to use the stairs." He inclined his chin. The gym was two stories high, but there were stairs on the edge that led to other workout rooms on the second level. "Two lengths of the gym, then ten flights of stairs. We'll repeat it a few times." It wasn't a question, and she could already tell it would be more than a few.

Cambree took off and tried to keep her chin up and her legs moving, even though they were quivering with exhaustion and the muscles in her neck and arms felt like they were seizing from the weight of the bucket. She wouldn't quit, though; she wanted to keep hearing Emmett say, "That's my girl, sweetheart, and you're a beast." The thought of disappointing him kept her pace up quicker than if she were in an official race.

Emmett could not believe how tough Cambree was. He put her through every event he'd ever seen done on a Warrior race, even having her use trees in the forest like a monkey to try to imitate the hanging Warrior. He made her do a lot of burpees and sprints and she was probably cussing him in her head, but she just kept going and going. He started worrying whether he could help her improve when she was already at a fitness level that was close to a lot of the professional athletes he'd competed with.

After they finished with the obstacles, he had her eat a protein bar and down a water bottle and a Gatorade. Then they took the workout into the weight room. He'd never been interested in a client like this and he hoped he wasn't transparent to everyone, especially Cambree, but he couldn't resist calling her "sweetheart" and "my girl." It just came naturally, and her funny responses made the day even better.

She was pulling a weighted rope against a cable machine, and he was in awe of the smooth muscle rippling in her arms.

"Your muscle tone is impressive. Maybe you should take up modeling instead of schoolteaching," he said.

Cambree rolled her eyes. "No-o-o way! I couldn't stand that fakey life." She hit the end of the cable length and released it.

"Do it again," Emmett said. "Watch your posture, keep that back straight and your shoulders down." She obeyed quickly. This girl was a perfect student.

"What's wrong with my 'fakey life'?" Britney asked.

Emmett looked to Tracy, who lifted her shoulders. They must've just come around from the free weight area. Emmett hadn't realized they were close enough to hear them. Britney was covered in sweat, her makeup running down her face and her blonde hair in a haphazard ponytail.

"Looks like you've been working hard," Emmett tried to deflect.

"Tracy's amazing," Britney said. "There won't be an ounce of fat on me after this week."

Cambree stood. "I don't think there's an ounce of fat on you right now."

"Ah, you're sweet." Britney's blue eyes gleamed. "Why wouldn't you want to be a model?"

Cambree shrugged. "I'm sorry, that came out wrong. I'm from a really humble background. I wouldn't fit in with people who are classy and wealthy. You're so polished and beautiful. I'm sure everyone loves you."

Emmett wanted to protest that Cambree had no clue how beautiful and confident she was. She could fit in with any group.

No, not fit in. Shine above anyone. Her lingo might shock some people, but not the people that mattered.

Britney's eyes went from shrewd to happy. "You're pretty enough to model, but I understand if you haven't been raised to associate with high rollers."

Cambree smiled. "It's really impressive to me, what you do."

"Thank you, love." Britney blew her a kiss.

"Let's grab a drink, then head back to the free weights," Tracy said.

Britney gave them a jaunty wave and Emmett a seductive wink before strutting off. Emmett turned to face Cambree, not wanting an eyeful of Britney's cheeks. "You sell yourself short," he said.

Cambree shook her head. "No. I would never fit in with wealth and prestige." She dropped down to a seated position and grabbed the rope. "Again?"

Emmett nodded, but his head was swirling. He was impressed with how Cambree had handled Britney with poise and kindness, but he didn't like that she thought she wouldn't fit in with the wealthy elite. He didn't think of himself as a high roller, but he and his brothers were high-profile billionaires and he was a well-known athlete. He'd dated some actresses and models but never gotten serious with any of them. Did Cambree think that was his crowd? He wasn't sure how to ask without showing how interested he was in her. He shouldn't be considering dating Cambree. He could just imagine the field day the media would have about him falling for a fitness camp participant, especially if her background was really as humble as she seemed to think it was. He watched Cambree pull on the rope. She bit at her lip, and she was so cute—no, beautiful. Who could blame him for wanting to fall?

CHAPTER FOUR

Cambree worked hard through the first day of torture, not sure how she would do it again tomorrow. Emmett was fun and he really knew his stuff.

As she pulled through a set of seated rows on the cable machine, she felt his hand on her upper back. She gulped, feeling much warmer than she should be from the workout. His large palm pressing against her thin shirt was intoxicating.

"Keep that back straight, and I want you to concentrate on squeezing your shoulder blades together."

"Got it," she muttered, unable to think of an intelligent response with him touching her like that. She had to remind herself he was simply instructing her, not trying some romantic move, but it was hard to remember that.

They moved slowly through the exercises. He really concentrated on building strength and power by focusing on the eccentric or lowering phase of each lift. She was lowering into a dead lift when he touched her hamstring muscle.

Cambree jumped and straightened quickly, whirling to face him. "Those are my legs!" she cried out.

Emmett's eyes were wide and he backed up, lifting his hands up. "I ... it's part of me training you. I have to make sure you're doing the exercise right."

"What on the green earth would make you need to touch my thigh like that?" It had felt so stinking good that she could hardly talk straight right now.

"I was checking how your hamstring was responding, and it isn't as tight as I'd like it. You're cheating and not keeping your back flat enough, so your hamstring isn't getting as intense of a workout." He shook his head. "I wasn't trying to touch you inappropriately."

She swallowed hard, her face flaming red. "I'm sure you didn't mean nothing by it, it's just ... your hands, whew! They're smokin', you know?"

Emmett's eyes got even wider. "Oh."

Man, she'd made this awkward. She tried to fix it. "I mean, I've worked with other trainers, but they never made me go hot and cold all over when they touched me."

Emmett pushed a hand through his hair. "Okay."

She closed her eyes and wanted to crawl in a hole.

"Are you okay with me touching you ... if it helps with your training?"

Cambree nodded, not able to look at him. *Keep your fat mouth shut and work*, she told herself.

They went through some more lifts and she was able to stay quiet and not embarrass herself. When she was doing pull-ups, she made it to fifteen before her grip started giving out. Emmett wrapped his arms around her thighs and said, "Let's go, sweetheart. You got this."

He'd just said "sweetheart" again. Oh, my, he was much too cute. And now he was touching her again. She was sweaty and gross and needed to keep her head focused on the workout, but his hands touching her legs made her stomach swirl and her mouth go dry, and she about lost her grip on the bar. She kept going because he was cheering her on. "You got this."

Cambree made it through twenty more assisted pull-ups before he let her go and she dropped to her feet. Emmett high-fived her, but instead of letting go, he wrapped his hand around hers. "You rocked that. That's my girl."

Butterflies swirled in Cambree's stomach as his large hand surrounded hers and she stared into his handsome face. She licked her lips and his eyes dropped to her lips, then met hers again.

"Where did you get your blue eyes?" he asked.

"My daddy."

He nodded, then whispered so quietly she barely heard it, "Beautiful."

Neither of them moved. The way he stared at her made her stomach smolder and made her feel like she was beautiful to him. Cambree had never felt such sparks, desire, or pull to a man before, including her ex-fiancé.

A movement at the gym door broke them apart. Cambree should've been grateful. Emmett was an amazing trainer, but she could never allow herself to fall for a richie man again and wasn't sure how she was going to make it out of this camp with her heart intact. Especially if he kept giving her those lingering looks.

Emmett cleared his throat. "Ready for more obstacles?"

"Point me the way to torture, bossy man."

Emmett chuckled and grabbed the weighted bucket. They

went through a lot of the Warrior obstacles again. Of course, he kept throwing burpees and sprints in there. To cool down before dinner, he took her on another six-mile run.

Cambree smiled. She hurt, but she loved being pushed to her limit and she really loved being around Emmett. He didn't act like any of the upper-class people she'd met before. Granted, the only ones she'd met before were Nolan and his snooty crowd. Part of the reason she talked the way she did was because of how much Nolan had hated it and how she'd tried to change for him when they dated. He'd treated her like a princess in some ways but expected her to be something she wasn't. Then he'd dumped her and broken her heart regardless of how hard she tried. She shook it off, telling herself she was over it and she would stay true to herself and her upbringing no matter how impressive a man was.

She showered quick, put on minimal makeup and a comfortable T-shirt dress, and went to meet everyone for dinner. The dinner was delicious with salmon, chicken breast, and a huge variety of veggies and salads. Everyone got their food and Cambree found herself seated between Britney and Lucy.

"Why don't you eat some real food, you rabbit?" Lucy asked.

Cambree looked down. Her plate was filled with a huge variety and she'd just taken a bite of sweet potato that was delicious.

"Not you. Her." Lucy pointed at Britney.

Britney sucked in a breath and bit at her lip, pushing some of the dry salad around on her plate. "You don't understand how it is. If I gain a pound, I could lose everything."

Cambree remembered her own comment earlier about not wanting a model's lifestyle, and it was dead-on for more reasons than having to act perfect all the time. "You really need some protein, though, to maintain the muscle and help you work hard again tomorrow," Cambree said gently, and her heart went out to Britney.

"I'll try a little chicken." Britney stood, and Cambree noticed the three male trainers and Troy watching as she walked over to the food. Her skirt wasn't quite as short as her shorts had been earlier, but Cambree still dreaded the thought of her leaning forward.

Cambree's gaze swung to Emmett. He watched her, not Britney. "Thank you," he mouthed.

Cambree nodded, not quite sure if he was grateful she'd gotten Britney to eat more or grateful she'd stemmed a fight between Lucy and Britney.

Dinner was pretty quiet, mostly the trainers joking with Gunner. The participants were all exhausted.

"Nana Lucy lost her snark halfway through the afternoon," Mark told the group.

"You're gonna lose more than that if you keep trying to kill me," Lucy flung back at him.

They all laughed.

"Tough first day?" Emmett asked.

"You have no idea. I wish my legs would fall off and never come visit again."

"I was impressed with how tough you all were today." Emmett smiled at Cambree.

"He's only impressed with our Warrior woman," Lucy said, winking at Cambree.

Cambree blushed and took a bite of salmon. It melted in her mouth and she was grateful that she could eat as much healthy food as she liked. Her sport didn't require her to be at some perfect weight.

After dinner, they went through a routine of massage, ice baths, and rolling out their muscles on foam rollers. The spa was exactly what Cambree had dreamed a spa should be: smelling of lavender and eucalyptus with lovely music and smiling attendants. She even got a facial with Lucy and Britney. Britney had been right that being pampered was fabulous.

As they finished, they were instructed to get in their suits and meet up with their trainers at the swimming pool. Emmett stood by the diving board in a T-shirt and swim trunks.

"A low-intensity workout will help you not be sore tomorrow so we can keep working hard," Emmett explained. "Does everyone know how to swim?"

They all nodded. "But I stink at it," Lucy said.

Emmett smiled. "That's all right. You can swim some slow laps or even just tread water or walk in the shallow end and circle your arms through the water. This pool is salt water, so it almost works like an Epsom salt bath and will help you feel better in the morning."

"I'm going to sleep like a freaking baby," Lucy muttered. "But I might not get out of bed in the morning."

"Don't worry, Nana Lucy, I'll come wake you up," Mark teased her.

"If only you were my age," Lucy said with an exaggerated sigh.

Cambree peeled off her swimsuit cover-up and dropped it on a chair. The pool area was every bit as gorgeous as the rest of the resort. The Olympic-sized pool had two infinity hot tubs perched above the shallow end with water spilling over into the pool. The backdrop was trees and the blue Texas sky, and there were gorgeous flower arrangements and huge pots filled with bright blooms scattered throughout the pool area.

"Those hot tubs are calling my name," Lucy said as she gingerly moved down the steps into the pool. She looked classy and fit in a pale blue one-piece suit that flattered her beautiful complexion.

"You said it, sister." Cambree's body ached. The massage, ice bath, and rolling had helped, but right now she'd rather soak in one of those hot tubs and watch the sun set and then sleep for twelve hours. Her legs stiffened as she descended the steps into the pool. The pool was lukewarm, and as she sank into the water, she released a sigh. It was almost as good as a hot tub.

She caught Troy staring at her and closed her eyes to avoid having to respond. He was such a creeper.

"Holy mother of Hades," Lucy murmured.

Cambree chuckled. She stared at the older lady, thinking she'd found a kindred spirit. "What?"

Lucy didn't say anything—she simply pointed. Emmett had taken off his shirt and he stood at the edge of the pool, ready to dive in, but Britney had detained him. There was so little fabric on Britney's suit that Cambree wasn't sure it could qualify as swimwear, but it was Emmett that captured all of her attention. His chest was broad and tan and perfectly muscled. His shoulders and biceps were so shredded, they took Cambree's breath away. She could hardly let herself look at his perfect abs; they were like steps she wanted to walk her fingertips up. He was glorious.

"He has better lines than a Dodge Charger," she whispered.

Lucy dug her fingernails into Cambree's arm. "I watched you two most of the day to get my mind off my misery. If you care for the elderly female population like yours truly who will never have a man like that look twice at them, please, please hit on that man and kiss him for me this week."

Cambree laughed and shook her arm free. "I'd happily comply, but a richie like that is never going to be interested in me." She plunged under the water, then started breast-stroking toward the deep end.

Lucy had claimed she couldn't swim, but she was right by Cambree's side, doggy-paddling ferociously. "If you believe that, you are du-umb for real. I've watched two of my sons find the love of their lives, and neither of them looked at their sweethearts with any less interest than I've seen him looking at you today." Lucy headed for the nearest wall as Cambree continued swimming. When Lucy grabbed on the wall, she turned around and yelled, "Do the right thing! Do it for the women of the world!"

Cambree laughed and swam toward the deep end. The pool was so big, there was plenty of room for all of them to swim around. Gunner and Troy were treading water while talking to Tracy. Gunner caught her eye and grinned and waved. Cambree smiled at him, but her attention was drawn back to Emmett. She hated the stirring of jealousy she felt as Britney pressed her barely covered chest into his arm.

Emmett stepped away from Britney and dove into the water. Watching him move was truly beautiful. Cambree wanted to go back and re-watch all of his football games. He surfaced close to Gunner and chatted with him for a while before ducking under the water again. He swam strong freestyle strokes until he was at her side.

Cambree treaded water easily and smiled at him. "Thanks. This feels marvelous."

"It's my favorite thing after a hard workout."

"Wait. How did you fit in a workout today? I thought your focus was on killing me."

Water sparkled off his handsome face, and some droplets were caught in the short hair of his beard. "While you were getting pampered, Beau helped me lift." He tilted his head. "Do you want to swim a few laps?"

"Sure, but I'm feeling pretty slow right now."

He chuckled. "I haven't seen you do anything slow today." With that, he took off with freestyle, and she couldn't resist pursuing him. They raced the length of the pool a few times, then changed to breaststroke and talked as they slowly traversed the pool. The sun sank behind the trees to the west, and Cambree realized everyone else had disappeared.

"Hey, you two," Lucy called from the pool deck. "We're all going to shower, then meet at my cabin for contraband sugar at ten. You in?"

"She's teasing, right?" Emmett asked.

"I doubt it." Cambree raised her voice. "Count me out. I need my shut-eye."

"Don't forget what you promised me." Lucy pumped her eyebrows and slowly walked away.

"What did you promise her?" Emmett stopped in the shallow end and pulled his hands behind his back, stretching his chest.

Cambree's mouth went dry and her pulse jumped. "I didn't promise her a snitching thing. She's mental." There was no way she was telling him about Lucy's crazy idea of the two of them getting together. The prince and Cinderella were a fairy tale she'd aspired to at one time. Now she knew that only brought pain.

Emmett studied her. The lights in the pool and on the patio flickered across his face and glorious chest. "Are you going straight to bed, or do you want to soak in the hot tub for a bit?"

"Those hot tubs are like sirens—they've been calling my name all evenin'."

"You'd better try them out, then." He gestured in front of him with a smile.

Cambree was grateful she was wearing a sporty Nani suit that fully covered her rear and her chest. There was a strip of her abdomen that showed, but she felt confident and pretty in the floral suit. Her body was nothing like Britney's with Barbie-like curves, but Emmett's quick glances suggested that he liked her shape.

They walked side by side to the hot tub. Emmett took her hand and helped her down the steps. The warmth of his touch seemed twenty degrees hotter than the warm water of the hot tub. When she'd been lifting today, he'd touched her quite a bit. She'd forced herself not to dwell on how fabulous his touch felt and not get caught up in his spell. They were worlds apart socially, and she couldn't let herself get pulled in like she had with Nolan.

He released her hand and they both sank down into the perfect warmth.

Cambree closed her eyes and leaned her head back. "Now *this* is what I'm talking about." She did a little dance with just her arms in the air.

Emmett chuckled. "It's the perfect end to a hard day."

Cambree opened her eyes and studied his handsome face. "Today was a cakewalk," she said, but she immediately regretted it.

"Oh really? You'd better lace up your bootstraps for tomorrow, then."

Cambree giggled. "I meant the day was fun and I liked it.

The workouts were horrendous and tough, and you're the meanest trainer I've ever worked out with."

Emmett gave her a challenging look. "I see the backpedaling now. You're not going to sleep tonight, you'll be so scared for tomorrow."

"My belly is a-shaking with fear. You only had half a day to destroy me today."

"You're a pretty tough lady. I can imagine you'll just say, 'Bring it on'."

"Thanks. Truly, don't go easy on me, but I am petrified thinking what tomorrow might bring."

"You should be, but at least we'll be together," Emmett said.

There was a promise in his dark eyes that both thrilled and terrified her. Together? They weren't together. It didn't matter that she would've liked to explore that option; she wasn't opening herself up to the suffering of loving a high-society man again.

She looked around the empty pool area. "I didn't even notice everybody else leaving."

"So caught up in me?"

The hot tub was suddenly very hot. Emmett Hawk was flirting with her. Her! Little Cambree Kinley from a trailer park in Colorado. She met his gaze and felt like she was floating in heat and joy and the opportunity to maybe honor Lucy's wishes and kiss this fine specimen of a man. Could she enjoy the moment without giving up her heart?

Remembrance came like a shot of cold water from the irrigation hose aimed straight up her nose. Nolan. He'd ruined her heart for any kind of relationship, especially with someone who was wealthy and famous.

Cambree broke from his gaze and pushed herself out of the

water. "I'd better go check my eyelids for holes. Thanks for beating me up today."

"Sure. See you in the morning."

"Six a.m.?" He'd explained to all of them they needed at least eight hours of sleep.

He smiled. "If Nana Lucy doesn't nail my cabin door shut tonight so she can sleep in."

Cambree giggled, remembering Lucy threatening to do a lot worse than that. "See you when it's dark and early."

She found a towel stack on a nearby table and wrapped up, grabbing her cover-up and slipping into her flip-flops. As she walked toward the gate that would lead her to the clearing and her cabin, she glanced back. Emmett sat on the edge of the hot tub, watching her go. She loved the figure he cut with his beautiful body and handsome face, but she didn't love everything he represented. He'd been born and bred to a different life than she could ever lead. He was a Hawk brother, for crying out loud. They personified beautiful perfection. She would never fit in with him and his family.

She turned and trudged away, hoping she could sleep without dreaming of him.

CHAPTER FIVE

The entire group was pretty quiet and slow on the run the next morning. Emmett's knee was aching, but he ignored it. Cambree had stuck close to Britney this morning, which was probably the only way to guarantee that he wouldn't get close to her. It bothered him, but he shook it off and ran next to Gunner. They talked football and Emmett really liked the kid's positive attitude. He hoped the kid made it to the NFL next year. The main thing that worried him was Gunner's size. He had decent height, but he was pretty thin. He had an unconquerable spirit, though, and ate up everything Emmett told him about putting on size.

After the run, they ate breakfast then went with their individual trainers for the morning workout. Emmett was excited and a little apprehensive to show Cambree the surprise he'd thought of late last night and luckily got workers here early this morning to put in place. His brothers and dad would probably think it was a waste of money, but it could be used until he finished with fitness camps, and when this place reverted to a high-scale resort they could call it a children's play area. Maybe.

"You ready?" he asked Cambree.

"As I'll ever be." She looked hesitant, though. He'd pushed her hard yesterday, but he already knew she had one of those unconquerable spirits that could work through tough things. He thought of his knee and wondered if he could somehow push through it.

He started her out lifting some free weights, then using the cable machines, before they headed to the gym to start replicating obstacles she'd be facing on race day. It was exhilarating to run some of the sprints with her. Even though it hurt his knee, it made him remember how it felt to fly across the field. He hated to think he'd never be back there.

They went outside with only a little time to spare before lunch. Cambree headed for the wooded area where the workers had been instructed to replicate some obstacles for her. As they came around the trees, Emmett smiled. The workers had been quick and efficient. There were inverted climbing walls, monkey bars, and a bunch of ropes for hanging from and climbing on attached to the trees. Three of the toughest obstacles in the Warrior circuit.

Cambree stared at everything. Eventually, she turned to him, her eyes wide. "How did you ...?" She shook her head, then jumped at him, wrapping her arms around his neck and giving him a fierce hug. "Thank you!"

Emmett laughed and held her close for much too short of a time. "If I'd known I'd get this response, I would've done it sooner."

Cambree focused those blue eyes on him, and time stuttered. She looked like she was going to say something, but then she pulled back, shaking her head. "How did you get this set up so quickly?"

"I know a contractor, and he found some used play equipment and got it installed this morning."

"I love it!" She squealed and clapped her hands together, but then her face drooped. "You didn't waste a fat load of cash, did you? You can ... reuse all this for something other than my training?"

"Oh yeah," he hastened to reassure her. "I just realized yesterday when you were hanging from tree branches that we needed more accessible equipment for you."

"You're a rock star." She bit at her lip and looked so cute and kissable, Emmett almost bent down and tasted those naturally pink lips.

Luckily—or maybe unluckily—he remembered he was her trainer when she pushed out a breath and said, "Well, put me to work, bossy man."

Emmett grinned, then started barking out orders, and she followed them perfectly. He wondered how badly it would really reflect on him if he fell in love with a training camp participant. He could wait until camp was over to officially date her. The media still might harass him, but it would be worth it to be with Cambree. No matter their differences in background, not even his dad or Callum could blame him for being drawn in by Cambree. He knew his mom, Creed, and Bridger would adore her. Why should their social status, family background, or financial level matter?

Cambree pushed through another excruciating physical day. Emmett had been right that the swimming and massages would help them be not as sore, but she still had some stiff muscles and Emmett slammed her even harder today than he had yesterday. She'd been half in love with him by last night, and the climbing equipment and walls he'd had installed this morning about pushed her into full-on love. She kept scolding herself and trying to keep away from him emotionally, protect her still-aching heart. But when he'd held her close after her impromptu thank-you hug, she thought Nana Lucy had a brilliant idea to get a kiss this week. After all, how could she tell Lucy no?

After lunch, they had a break from workouts while Tracy taught them about clean eating and how to avoid fads in nutrition. It was nice to sit and learn for a bit, but then it was back to work as usual. Cambree didn't mind, because she got to be with Emmett.

As they walked out of the dining area, she heard Troy mutter, "Emmett Hawk gets a piece of everything hot."

She looked over her shoulder and glared when she saw Troy leering at her. He lifted his chin and shot her a smile that looked more like a sneer. Then he puckered his lips in an exaggerated kissing motion.

Cambree whirled back around and glanced at Emmett, who was shooting daggers at Troy. When Troy finally looked at him, Emmett said, "Watch it."

Troy turned away and didn't answer. Cambree wondered if Emmett would go after him, but he took her elbow and they walked away together. Neither said anything about it, but the unwanted interaction cast a pall over their afternoon workout. Cambree didn't like the way Troy looked at her, and the way he'd said Emmett could get anything hot made her feel cheap and gross.

The massages and spa time were fabulous but swimming didn't go quite as well that night because Beau set up an impromptu game of water polo. They all had a great time learning and playing the game, but Cambree didn't get any alone time with Emmett. She should've been relieved—she knew her heart couldn't take falling in love with another wealthy guy, and especially a famous Hawk brother—but she was drawn to Emmett like a honey bee to an exquisite flower. Troy was absent from swimming, which was fine by her. Gunner said Troy was worn out and wanted to get some more rest tonight.

They all left the pool area together after they tired of water polo. Cambree caught Emmett's eye, and he mouthed, "Hot tub?" and gestured with his head.

She smiled and nodded. Her self-control had been all used up working so hard physically, and she didn't know how to tell Emmett no. She walked with the group toward her cabin and said her goodnights. Dropping off her swimsuit cover-up inside, she drained a water bottle, giving the group a little time to each get to their own cabins. She wanted Emmett all to herself, no matter how unwise it was.

When she walked out of her cabin door, she was only wearing her swimsuit flip-flops. She felt daring, like she was sneaking off to meet a boy without her mama's permission. She laughed at herself. She was a full-grown adult and her mama would love Emmett ... but then again, her mama had loved Nolan, up until he'd humiliated and dumped Cambree.

She passed Lucy's cabin and could hear voices and laughter inside. She wouldn't put it past Lucy to have smuggled treats into the camp. The food was so good here, though, and they even had fruit, sorbet, and some dark chocolate for dessert. Cambree didn't need any extra treats. Being with Emmett in the hot tub sounded delicious enough for her.

She had passed two more cabins when a hand suddenly clamped over her mouth and she was dragged behind the last cabin and shoved against the exterior wall. Her heart pounded in her ears as the wood of the cabin wall scratched against her bare back.

The light from the cabins illuminated Troy's face. His eyes were stormy and not completely clear. His breath smelled like alcohol. "Beautiful Cambree. Britney was a lot of fun last night, definitely more my type, but I wanted to see why Emmett Hawk is so drawn to you. Don't get me wrong, you're hot, but white trash isn't usually what I'm into."

He had one of her arms pinned, but Cambree was able to hit at him with her free hand. She tried to wrench her mouth free so she could scream for help and then tell him where to go.

"You can fight if you want to." He grinned. "Even the ones who fight love what I have for them."

Gross. Cambree pushed against his shoulders with her hand and squirmed to free herself, but he wasn't budging. He pulled his hand away from her face and bent to kiss her. She spit in his face and brought her knee up quick. Troy groaned, and she was able to shove him away and dodge out from under his arm. He dove at her, tackling her into the grass. Cambree screamed.

Troy forcefully rolled her over and glared down at her. He yanked her swimsuit off her shoulder, and Cambree cried out when his rough hands pressed over her tender skin.

"Stop, Troy!" she cried. "You'll be thrown in the pen for this."

Ice formed in the pit of her stomach as he stared at her like he didn't even care what repercussions would come his way. "Nobody's going to believe you didn't want this."

"Help!" she screamed, terror making her hair stand on end.

Cambree heard footsteps pounding their direction, and her heart lifted with hope. *Please let it be someone who can help*. Troy straightened up, still sitting on her and pushing her into the hard ground with his body weight.

An arm shot into her line of vision and roughly lifted Troy off of her. Scrambling to her feet and pulling her swimsuit back on, she watched as Emmett slammed Troy into the cabin wall, then released him and hit him several times in the face and gut. The taut, striated muscles in Emmett's back and arms worked in synchrony to protect her from Troy.

Troy cowered and begged, "Stop, man! What the freak?"

"You tell me, Troy," growled Emmett, grabbing Troy's shirt with both hands. "What the freak?"

"It's cool. Just having a little fun. Every girl wants a piece of a football star." Troy's bloody mouth twitched in a half grin. "I know *you* know what I'm talking about."

"You're disgusting," spat Emmett. "Prison's too good for scum like you."

"No!" Troy's cry of anguish was pitiful. "I'll never play in the NFL. Please."

Emmett grunted out a disgusted laugh. "You just assaulted Cambree. You think I care about your NFL hopes?"

Troy glared at Cambree. "I should've stuck to the supermodels, not wasted my time with trash."

Cambree flinched. Troy was a scum-ball, but what if some part of Emmett agreed with him?

Emmett gripped Troy with one hand and slammed his fist

into his gut with the other. Troy hollered out and dropped to the ground. Emmett bent down close. "You're the trash."

Troy only wheezed in reply.

"Stay down," Emmett growled. He looked glorious and intimidating, standing over Troy with his bare chest trembling with restrained rage. "Unless you want to get thrashed."

Troy didn't move.

Emmett yanked his phone out. "Beau," he barked. "Get the police here and come out to the open area now."

Cambree adjusted her swimsuit, making sure it covered her fully, and backed up a few steps, not wanting to be anywhere near Troy. Truthfully, Emmett was a little bit scary right now too.

Emmett glanced at her, and his rigid face and body softened. "You okay?"

She nodded quickly, biting at her cheek to keep the tears from coming. She'd had unwanted attention before, but no one had ever grabbed her like that. It had never been more than verbal innuendos.

Beau ran up to them and took in the scene quickly. Jacob was right on his heels. Emmett dragged Troy up off the ground and toward Beau, thrusting the younger man at him. "Take him into my office and we'll meet with the police. He'll be well-behaved because he doesn't want this to go any worse for him, right, Troy?"

Troy nodded, not looking at any of them. He stalked toward the main building with Beau and Jacob right on his heels.

Emmett turned to Cambree. All the fire she'd seen in him when he was pummeling Troy disappeared. "Ah, Cam." He opened his arms to her.

Cambree gave a little sigh of relief and went right into his arms. The nickname he'd just used was so tender that she wondered if he was falling for her as hard and fast as she was for him. He smelled like chlorine and salt from the swimming pool, and she was all too aware of him in nothing but his swim trunks. She shuddered and clung to his bare back, kneading her fingers into the glorious muscle there. Muscle that had just protected her from Troy. No one had ever protected her like that, and right now he was a bastion of strength and safety.

Emmett groaned. "What did he do to you, sweetheart?"

Cambree swallowed and forced herself to meet his gaze and be strong. "He grabbed me and pushed me up into the cabin wall. I kneed him and almost got away, but then he tackled me and tried to—he touched me—" She shook her head, her stomach churning. "Then you came. Thank you."

He nodded, much too somber and worried about her.

"I'm okay," she said, but anyone could read through her tone of voice—she definitely wasn't okay. She forced herself to pull away from his embrace, though it was the last thing she ever wanted to do, and gnawed at her lip. "I want to go shower." Emmett's arms had replaced the filthy feeling of being pawed at by Troy, but she wanted to just shower it all away and hopefully go to sleep. Would she be able to sleep remembering being held against her will and the fear that she couldn't get away? Troy had been so strong, and she hated that he'd touched her.

"You'll probably have to talk to the police first," Emmett gently reminded her.

Cambree wrapped her arms around herself, chilled even though it was a warm summer night.

"The police might take a minute, though. We're not exactly close to town. Shall we go grab your swimsuit cover-up and then get you a hot cocoa or cup of coffee while we wait?" Emmett asked.

"You have cocoa at the elitist fitness camp?" She tried to smile, but it fell flat.

"Oh yes, ma'am. This is a five-star resort when it's not a fitness camp; we have all manner of illegal contraband like hot cocoa." He held out his hand and Cambree loved how nonthreatening and kind this huge man could be. She was sure Troy would never describe him as nonthreatening, but Emmett was one of those good old boys who would never hurt a woman. Cambree could easily sense that. The fact that he knew she'd want to cover up before the police came made her feel like they were much closer than they actually were.

She placed her hand in his, and the comfort of his large hand around hers sent warmth up her arm. They fell into step together and Emmett walked her to her cabin, where she hurriedly threw her cover-up on, and then he escorted her around the side of the huge wraparound porch to the kitchen and dining area.

"You have very ... large hands." She'd wanted to say nice or perfect, but things were already getting far too intimate with him protecting her.

He chuckled. "Wide receivers need to be fast and have good hands."

She glanced askance at him. "Good hands. Yes, you definitely do."

He pulled the door open and held it for her. Cambree let him lead her inside and make her a cup of cocoa, which she had trouble getting down before the police came. She wished she would've been able to give him a kiss of gratitude or ask him to hold her close with those good hands of his, but after being grabbed by Troy, nothing felt right and she just wanted this night to be over.

CHAPTER SIX

Emmett noticed from the moment Cambree walked out of her cabin, and as they went on their morning run with the group, that she had not recovered from last night. Who could blame her? The only way he could relate was remembering being a young child and Callum or Creed would pin him down and laugh at him, but he knew they had no evil intent. His brothers were competitive, tough, and intense, but none of them were deliberately hurtful. He could remember lots of wrestling growing up and sometimes all-out brawls, but if somebody cried uncle, the other brother would let them go. Cambree had cried for help and for Troy to stop, and he'd hurt her physically and emotionally.

He'd overheard Troy tell the police that he just wanted a piece of the "sweet action" that Emmett Hawk was getting. Nothing Troy said should bother him, but he'd seen the way Troy had leered at Cambree the past two days, and he knew Troy was one of those guys who wanted to prove he was better than

Emmett. It made sense he would go after the woman Emmett was obviously interested in. That made him feel like the attack was Emmett's fault, and he couldn't stomach that. How could he protect Cambree and make the nightmare from last night go away?

They finished their run and broke off in pairs to workout. Even Lucy had been quiet on their run, and no one asked where Troy and Jacob had disappeared to. Emmett had given Jacob a paid week off since his client was gone. This adult fitness camp idea was worse than a flop. The youth camps were a lot more work, but not emotionally challenging like this. Emmett had more youth camps scheduled through the summer, and they were all booked with waiting lists. Maybe he should just focus on youth, but what would be his excuse come fall about not playing football?

He started Cambree out with some light weight lifting, focusing on a lot of pull-ups and lifts that imitated climbing and holding and moving her own body weight. After a couple of hours, he gave her a break for a snack and sports drink. They hadn't talked much, and he didn't know what to say to her now. *Sorry Troy is a jerk and tried to assault you?* He didn't know how to empathize, but he hoped his sympathy was perceived as genuine. Troy would face attempted rape charges, and he deserved the stiffest sentence in Emmett's mind.

After the snack, they went outside and trained on the obstacle course he'd had made for her. Yesterday afternoon he'd had them add another climbing wall that was smooth with no handholds.

Cambree tried to climb up the smooth wall but missed her handhold at the top and slipped back down.

"It's okay, you got this," Emmett encouraged.

She didn't look at him and tried the wall again, with not much better results. Emmett didn't know if he should encourage or instruct, but he'd Googled her and seen her do this very obstacle in the middle of a race when she was already exhausted and she'd conquered it then.

"You okay?" he asked tentatively.

"No, I'm not okay," she threw back at him. "And stop being so stinking nice!"

Emmett reared back. "I'm sorry?"

"No, *you* can't be sorry." She paced in front of him. "Yell at me. Make me do burpees. Make me do sprints. But don't treat me like I'm a china doll!" She rounded on him. "Do you realize you haven't made me do burpees or sprints all day today?"

"Well, I ..." There was no excuse. He was going easier on her today, but what was he supposed to do? How was he supposed to act?

She shook her head. "No, it's not you, it's me. I'm a crackpot mess." She went back to pacing.

"Anyone would be, being attacked like that."

She pursed her lips together. "I realize I'm a simple girl, but I always believe the best of everybody. My mama says it's my gift." She choked on a sob and Emmett wanted to pull her into his arms, but he didn't know if that was the right move at the moment. He wanted to gush about how great she was. She was *not* a simple girl. She was the most intriguing woman he'd ever met.

"It's an amazing gift," he said quietly. "I've noticed that you're kind to everyone, even Britney."

"I'm sure Britney has a reason for acting the way she does, but Troy ..." She stopped pacing and bit at her lip. "How could that scum-ball think he had the right to ... ugh, I don't even want to think about it!"

Emmett waited a beat, then admitted, "I don't know how he could treat you like that." He really didn't. He'd been raised to respect others and his mom would never have tolerated any kind of behavior like that, especially toward a woman.

"You know what?" Cambree's eyes flashed fire and determination at him. "I won't let that idiot win."

He lowered his chin, not sure what she meant.

"I am *not* a victim. I'm tough mentally and physically. I will not allow Troy to get in my head and make me scared and make me feel weak. I won't do it."

Emmett blinked at her. She was exceptional. "You are the toughest person I have ever met."

Cambree's fierce stance softened. She stared at him for several seconds, then finally cracked a smile. "Now I know that's a heap of baloney. You philander with the best athletes in the world, and your own brother is an awesome Navy SEAL."

Emmett returned the smile. "I stand by what I said. Toughest. Person. Ever."

"Thanks, Emmett." She smiled almost shyly, and then her face shifted again. "Enough of this wasting time." With a warrior-type yell, she ran and vaulted herself up the wall.

"That's my girl!" Emmett hollered, punching both fists in the air.

She slid back down and he met her, wanting to lift her off her feet and swing her around, but she put out her hand for a high-five. He slapped her hand, willing to give her distance if that's what she needed.

"What next, Hawk?" she drawled.

He was falling so hard for her. “Sprint to the lake,” he barked out.

She laughed and then took off like a rocket. Emmett chased after her.

When they hit the lake, he commanded, “Drop and army crawl through the shallow water.”

“Yes!” Cambree did a cute little cheerleader jump, then quickly obeyed.

“That’s my girl.”

She grinned up at him, splashing through the water.

Cambree had her fire back. Emmett couldn’t have been more relieved. She was as impressive as anyone he’d ever met. Then a cold weight settled in his stomach. Would this tough woman think less of him for hiding the extent of his injury and forced retirement from the world? She was inspiring and didn’t seem to care what anyone thought, and here he had to toe the line with social niceties. Emmett watched this beautiful, impressive woman scurry through the shallow water on all fours. He’d reveal the truth to the world right here and now and deal with any repercussions on him and his family—if it would give him a chance with Cambree.

Cambree couldn’t believe how different she felt tonight as opposed to last night. She’d struggled sleeping and spent a lot of time praying the night before. The Lord had answered her prayers today, showing her that she was strong and she wasn’t destined to live her life in fear. Nolan had torn her confidence apart, made her doubt herself and her value. Warrior races and her faith had helped her recover, but sometimes she still felt like the piece of trash he'd told her she was. Troy attacking her and the ugly things he'd said had made her feel even lower.

She shook that off and remembered how great Emmett had been today. She'd loved the time spent pushing her body and proving that she was tough, but most of all, she loved being with Emmett. Still, what if Emmett wasn't any different than Nolan? Her gift of looking for the best in people told her that not every rich guy would dump her like yesterday's garbage when they realized she wasn't cut out for interacting with the rich and famous. Yet did she ever want to put herself in that position again? She'd be very careful walking around in the dark alone and without pepper spray or some kind of weapon after Troy's attack.

Was she willingly putting herself in a position to be emotionally hurt if she trusted Emmett? She rolled her eyes. It wasn't like Emmett had even asked her out or tried to kiss her or anything. Maybe this was the way he treated all the women he trained. That thought made her mad as a wolverine backed into a corner.

She'd just gotten out of the shower after swimming and thrown on a tank top and some cotton shorts. She wished she could've soaked in the hot tub with Emmett and chatted after the long, hard day, but Britney had cornered him and eventually Cambree had left to shower and get some rest. She needed it after last night. Today had been taxing emotionally and physically, even with the empowerment of knowing she wasn't going to allow herself to be a victim. Now if she could get past Nolan's degradation. It had only been two months, so she tried to be patient with herself.

A soft rap on her door brought her head up. She put on some mint lip gloss and finger-brushed her long hair before running to the door. With Troy gone, she wasn't afraid of who it might be.

Emmett stood there in all his glory. He was the best-looking man she'd ever seen on this side of a movie screen, and those guys were touched up and fake. There was so much depth to Emmett, even if he had been raised more like Nolan than she wanted to think about.

He smiled, his eyes roving over her freshly washed face and hair. "You look really pretty all natural."

Cambree pushed her hair away from her face. "The only way you've seen me is all natural."

Emmett leaned against the doorframe. "After this week is over, maybe you'll let me take you on a date where you put on a pretty dress and I put on a suit."

Cambree loved imagining him in a suit. Had Emmett Hawk just asked her on a date? She wanted to squeal in delight and call one of her sisters, but the thought of dating the superstar outside of this safe refuge made her stomach drop like she'd just leapt off the bridge into the Colorado River.

She raised her eyebrows instead of screaming yes and getting herself into faster rapids than the Colorado could boast. "Maybe. Let's see how the week goes, bossy man."

He chuckled, then inclined his head toward the forest trail that led to the lake. "Do you want to go on a short walk to ... loosen your legs up?"

"Ooh, is that code for 'I'm going to decimate your legs tomorrow'?" She grinned up at him. She wished it was code for *Let me take you on a picturesque walk and kiss you.*

"If I haven't decimated your legs the past three days, you're getting a full refund."

She laughed at that. "You've pretty much destroyed my entire body."

His eyes swept over her body. "If your body looks this good after being destroyed, I'd love to see what it looks like normally."

"Stop." She laughed and walked out of the cabin, absolutely loving him flirting with her. He fell into step beside her and they walked down the trail for a few minutes, simply enjoying being side by side and the warm, quiet night, crickets chirping and lightning bugs flashing.

"I'm so sorry," Cambree said, breaking the silence.

"You're sorry?" His eyes cut to her. "You did nothing wrong."

"I was grumpy with you today."

He laughed. "Yeah, you were a bit grumpy."

"Thanks for being honest."

"You had every right to be much worse than grumpy."

She thought about last night, being trapped under Troy's body, him grabbing her. "When you saved me, I was all out of whack. I should've been more grateful."

"No. You went through something traumatic. I'm just sorry it happened at all, that I didn't get there quicker. Really sorry pricks like Troy were ever born." He muttered the last part.

She whirled on him and grabbed on to his forearms, which were thick and roped with muscle. "How can you be so buff, yet so gentle?"

Emmett gave her a slow grin that made her knees go weak. "My mother raised me right."

"She most certainly did." Even though they were from different worlds, he had definitely been raised to be a gentleman. "My mama taught me something important too."

"Besides how to be the most impressive woman in the world?" Emmett brushed her hair over her shoulder, his fingers trailing along the bare flesh of her shoulder and making her stomach quiver.

How did she respond to a line that sweet? Especially from someone as rocking as Emmett? "Thank you." She looked down, then met his dark gaze and forced out the bravest line of her life: "She taught me I should always show gratitude. There's not much I could give you, seeing how you're wealthy, famous, and successful, but I could at least give you a kiss of gratitude." Would he think she was too forward? Some lowly girl trying to seduce him?

Emmett gave her a slow grin, and her stomach filled with butterflies. He wrapped his hands around her lower back and leaned in closer. He smelled clean, like a manly soap and dryer sheets.

Cambree ran her hands up his arms, then threaded them behind his neck. She lifted up onto her tiptoes, their mouths centimeters apart. Was she brave enough to cross the distance?

Emmett studied her with an irresistible smolder in his eyes. "You said you were giving the kiss of gratitude ... I'm waiting."

Cambree couldn't help but laugh, but the humor didn't ruin the moment—far from it. She loved that they could tease and laugh together. All of her concerns—misgivings about Emmett being wealthy and famous, the fact they lived states apart, and the worry of this just being a fling—were thrown to the back burner as she pressed her lips to his. The fireflies must've gone insane, because the night seemed to light up around them. His lips were firm, and though he let her initiate the kiss, he quickly took control and ignited every pleasure receptor in her lips.

The kiss was innocent and sweet, yet full of delicious promise and desire stronger than she'd ever experienced in her life. His hands moved over her back, bringing a low burn to her stomach. She reveled in the beautifully formed muscle that pressed against her in a protective embrace.

She could've gone on kissing him all night; sleep wasn't important to her at all, no matter how hard tomorrow would be. Regrettably, Emmett pulled away. He smiled down at her, then simply took her hand and started walking her back to her cabin. Neither of them said a word. Cambree was hesitant to break the spell surrounding them. She pushed reality away and savored his hand surrounding hers, the safety, excitement, and joy that Emmett Hawk brought to her life.

When they reached her cabin, he bent down and gave her a tender kiss. "Good night," he whispered against her lips.

Cambree blinked up at him. "It is a good night," she said.

He chuckled, then released her and stepped back. Cambree fumbled open her door and couldn't resist catching his gaze one more time before she slipped inside. Emmett Hawk. Had that really just happened? She pressed her hand to her heart and then to her lips. Tonight had been magical. She didn't want to let tomorrow, or more specifically next week, intrude.

CHAPTER SEVEN

Emmett felt like he could conquer the world when he woke up. He hadn't planned on finding the woman of his dreams at camp, but the good Lord had blessed him to meet and get to know Cambree and he wasn't going to kick a gift horse in the mouth. Cambree was unreal—tough, brave, funny, beautiful. She truly could be the one for him. He suddenly cared little about his knee and that he might never play another football game in his life. What did that matter if he had Cambree?

Everyone met in the open green area for the morning run. Emmett fell into step beside Cambree and lowered his voice. "Last night was the best night of my life."

She glanced sharply up at him. "You don't get out much, huh?"

He chuckled. "Not with someone as impressive as Cambree Kinley."

"You haven't taken me out yet, bossy man. We'll see if *I'm* impressed after that."

He grinned, loving her spice. Ideas formed in his mind for how he would impress her. It would have to wait until after camp, but they only had a few days left. "Can you wait until after camp for me to sweep you off your feet?"

"As long as you promise good nights like last night." She winked, and Emmett's chest swelled. It sounded like she'd loved the kiss as much as he had. He couldn't wait to keep on kissing her, but right now he needed to focus on training her and getting her ready for her next race. With her determination, athleticism, and grit, she could definitely take the number one spot.

They worked hard together all day. Emmett had no problem challenging her physically, but he loved calling her "sweetheart" and "my girl" and taking every opportunity to touch her firm muscles. She rewarded him with lots of smiles and teasing.

After the participants' spa time while Emmett worked out with Beau and then everyone swam together, the rest of the group headed to bed and Emmett and Cambree stole a few minutes alone in the hot tub.

Emmett wrapped his hands around her waist and lifted her onto his lap. "Your waist is so small I can fit my hands all the way around it."

She laughed. "It's your hands. They're massive."

Her face was close to his as the water swirled around them. Her firm body pressed against his chest, making his stomach smolder. "So here you are pretty much perfect to me, but I'm this giant with too big of hands?"

Cambree ran her palms along the musculature of his shoulders. "No, you're pretty much perfect. I don't mind awkwardly big hands."

He laughed and cradled her even closer. "As long as you like my lips, I don't really care how you feel about my big hands."

She bit at her lip, and it was all he could do to slow down the moment before the kiss. "Your lips are better than perfect in my book," she said.

His chest filled with warmth that had nothing to do with the hundred-degree water. "Good, because they're going to be connecting with your lips soon."

"I've been waiting like a pig for his dinner for that."

Emmett grinned at her unique lingo but didn't resist any longer. He captured her lips with his, and they proceeded to make magic as their lips danced together and he savored her being so close in his arms. After several minutes, he forced himself to pull back; being only in swimsuits was playing with a fire that he didn't want to consume them. Their relationship was new and fragile. He wanted it to stay pure and develop into something beautiful and committed, like his parents had. That meant no intimacy before marriage, no matter how tempted he was right now.

"We'd better get some rest. Tomorrow is going to be brutal." He wrapped his hands around her waist and lifted her onto the step.

Cambree stepped out of the hot tub and he followed. "More brutal than the past four days?"

"You'll see in the morning."

She laughed and grabbed a clean towel, tossing him one. They dried off, then wrapped the towels around themselves and slipped into their flip-flops. Emmett took her hand and walked her out of the pool area toward the cabins.

"Thank you," she said quietly.

Emmett glanced down at her. "For?"

"Being you."

"That's all I know how to be."

She smiled. "Thank you for respecting me and not taking advantage of me when your kiss makes my head so cloudy I would struggle to say no if you pushed me."

Emmett's eyebrows jumped. Cambree was a sweetheart clear through, but she was also honest to a fault. "I would never take advantage of you, Cam."

"I know that." She squeezed his hand. "And I love the nickname."

He couldn't resist bending down and kissing her. He kept it short, but he realized he could never get enough of her. Is this how it happened for other men? Only his brother Creed had a serious girlfriend, Kiera, and he claimed to love her and know it was going to last forever. Emmett had never felt that, never felt this. He didn't want to stop feeling it.

A wail came from the cabin next to Cambree's, shocking him out of his sappy thoughts. Emmett and Cambree glanced at each other, then broke into a jog.

Lucy's door popped open, and she almost ran into them. "Hey, lover-birds. Who's screeching out here?"

A muffled sob came next.

"Britney?" Cambree guessed.

Lucy gritted her teeth. "I got her. You two go make out some more."

Cambree glanced up at Emmett.

"You want to go help Lucy?" he asked. Even though it would mean no more kissing for him tonight, he hoped Cambree would go. Lucy didn't seem very patient with Britney.

Cambree nodded and arched up on tiptoes, kissing his cheek. "I'll let you know if we need you."

"Thanks." He released her hand and watched as they walked to Britney's door and knocked. He would've preferred to stay with Cambree, but she was the type of person who would help someone in need, even if that person in need was ... a bit dramatic.

The door swung open and he heard Britney give one more cry before throwing her arms around Cambree's neck. "My life is ruined," she moaned.

Cambree hugged her back. "How can we help?"

Emmett turned and walked away. Cambree had Britney under control as if she was dealing with one of her sixth-grade students. She was definitely the most impressive person he'd ever met. He grinned, mentally planning the date he would take her on after camp was over.

Cambree ushered Britney back into her cabin and they sat side by side on the leather couch. She wished she wasn't in a wet swimsuit, and she really wished she was still in Emmett's arms, but she wanted to help Britney if she could. She needed to clear her head from Emmett's mind-blowing kisses anyway. She was getting swept up much too fast, but didn't know how to slow this love train down. The scary thing was that she'd fallen for Nolan fast and hard, too, and look how that had turned out.

Lucy sat across from them in a chair. "What's going on?" she asked.

Britney brushed at the eyeliner smearing under her eyes. Luckily her fake eyelashes made it so no mascara was smearing. "I'm ruined," she muttered.

Cambree's gut twisted. Troy. He said he'd had his way with Britney the night before he attacked Cambree. "Troy?" she asked.

Britney stared at her. "What about him?"

"Did he ... attack you?"

"Oh." Britney shook her head. "No. We made out the first night of camp, but it was nothing."

Cambree's shoulders relaxed. "So what's going on?"

Britney twisted her hands together. Her gaze darted to Lucy and then to Cambree. "I came to this camp because I'm five pounds heavier than last year, and no matter how hard I work, I can't lose it." She sighed. "My agent told me if I don't lose it, I'll lose my contracts with *Sports Illustrated* and *Maxim*. I thought this camp would be my answer, but I've actually gained two pounds this week." She focused on Cambree. "Not to point fingers, but I took your advice to eat a little more than usual."

Cambree wasn't quite sure how to respond to that.

"What a load of bull crap," Lucy spit out. She gestured to Britney. "You are perfectly gorgeous. The reason you weigh a little more is because you're gaining more muscle. Throw your stupid scale away, fire your agent, and go be a supermodel if that's what you want to be."

Britney's eyes widened. She pushed back against the sofa and simply stared at Lucy. Cambree didn't know what to say to soften Lucy's words, and she didn't think she should soften them. Lucy was dead-on.

The silence lingered for a few more beats. Cambree pressed Britney's hand; at least she could back up Lucy. "Lucy is exactly right. You've got a perfect shape, a gorgeous face, and the sweetest smile ever. Weight shouldn't matter a bushel of beans, and I'm sure you can find an agent with a brain in his head who will only care about how fabulous you look and the contracts he can secure for you. Your agent answers to you, not the other way around."

Britney's mouth opened and closed. Her eyes glistened, and then tears spilled over. She hugged Cambree and then released her, jumped to her feet, and hurried over to hug Lucy. She stood in the middle of the room, looking back and forth between the two of them. "You two are the best. Thank you!" Her eyes narrowed. "Wait. You aren't just saying this to butter me up so I'll be your friend and you'll know someone famous, right?"

Lucy cackled. "I thought you'd gotten to know me a little bit this week. I never say anything to butter somebody up. And Cambree knows Emmett Hawk; she doesn't need any other famous friends."

Britney wrapped her arms around herself and squealed. "You're right! You would never do that, and Emmett Hawk is a little bit more famous than me."

Lucy lifted her eyebrows at Cambree.

Britney gave a self-satisfied nod. "I've been killing it this week with the workouts and I'm going to keep killing it, and when this camp is over, my agent is either going to be supportive of me or I'll find someone else." She grinned. "I love you both!" As Cambree and Lucy stood, Britney hugged each of them a few more times before they escaped her cabin.

Lucy walked with Cambree to her cabin door. "You know what? That felt good. I've hated Britney and what she represents because of jacktard Tim and who he cheated with, but none of that is Britney's fault. Yeah, she's a shallow drama queen who likes to show her butt cheeks off, but she's a person and deserves to be happy."

Cambree nodded. "You did amazingly fabulous, Lucy."

Lucy sized her up. "What about you? Falling in love with the gorgeous billionaire superstar, are we?"

Cambree hugged herself and grinned, though her worries

pricked as she thought of Emmett as the billionaire and superstar. He was both, and she hated that world, but she liked Emmett too much to let the outside world intrude just yet. "I can't seem to help diving off the cliff."

"Hey, nobody's blaming you. You two are both great. I wish you loads of happiness."

"You'll find happiness again too," Cambree said.

"Maybe. But I'm already happy. I've got my boys, my daughters-in-law, and my grandgirls. And I know that I can rock this fifty-year-old body as well, and I've got my moxie back. That's enough for right now. I'm not waiting around for any man." She winked and turned, strutting back to her cabin.

"Wow, girl, you own that strut," Cambree called out.

"You know it." Lucy laughed and waved.

Cambree really liked Lucy, and she was glad they could help Britney out. Only two days left of camp and they'd all return to real life. Would what she and Emmett were developing last past the shelter of this beautiful wooded spot? Sadly, she didn't think it would. Dread filled her gut. She wanted to enjoy the time with Emmett, but every minute she fell harder for him. Was she an idiot to let herself fall?

CHAPTER EIGHT

The next day passed much too quickly, and real life loomed around the corner. Cambree didn't let herself think about it too much and simply enjoyed being with Emmett—his solidness, his quiet teasing, the way he touched her as he helped her lift or pushed her to climb faster or hang from an obstacle longer. They laughed a lot, and she lived for the times when he would whoop and call her his girl.

After lunch, Emmett stood and announced, "A very good friend of mine has agreed to come speak to y'all today." He grinned around at the group, then strode to the door of the dining room.

He walked back in with a woman so beautiful and well-known that Cambree felt her stomach swoop with excitement to meet her. Yet as she took in the too-comfortable way this perfectly put together lady was clinging to Emmett's arm, her stomach dropped like a lead balloon.

Emmett brought the woman in front of everyone and

beamed down at her. "This is Avalyn Shaman, acclaimed psychiatrist, author, motivational speaker, and creator of Health for All." He smiled so proudly at her, Cambree's stomach felt sour and her neck tight. "You can just call her Ava Baby for short."

Avalyn swatted at his shoulder playfully and laughed. "Please don't let that nickname get out." She turned to all of them with a full smile. She was an exotic beauty, definitely from some Arabic background with her high cheekbones, full lips, creamy brown skin, and silky dark hair.

"I don't think any of us needed the introduction," Gunner murmured. When Avalyn turned her smile on him, he added, "Forgive us if we stare, ma'am. We're all a bit starstruck."

"Can I get a selfie right now?" Lucy asked. "You're my hero!"

"Thank you so much," Avalyn said smoothly. Everything about her was smooth—her hair, her skin, and her red silky dress.

Cambree couldn't really process that Emmett still had his hand on this woman's lower back and was grinning at all of them like he was displaying his top prize. He caught Cambree's gaze and winked at her. Cambree pasted on her own smile, but jealousy ripped through her, making her hands clammy and her throat ache. Emmett and Avalyn looked perfect together—exquisite, really. As soon as she thought that, she realized she had seen them together on some magazine cover. If she remembered right, they'd been promoting Avalyn's world health incentives for clean water and healthy food for children.

She wanted to get out her phone and Google their names. Were they dating? It couldn't be possible. Emmett wouldn't be kissing Cambree if he was dating someone else. Would he? She'd heard many Hollywood stars paired up with whoever they were on set with, and then after filming went back to their spouse or partner without missing a beat. Just another reason she would never want to be part of some immoral, high-society world. She couldn't imagine Emmett was like that, but did she really know him well enough to know?

"You've all worked so hard this week," Emmett was saying. "But come next week, you'll be working out without your favorite trainer."

"I'll cry for you, Mark," Lucy called out.

Mark made a heart with his hands.

"We want you to go home motivated to keep giving every day, every workout your all. Avalyn is here to keep your head in the game."

"Thank you, Emmett." She beamed at him, then clapped her slender fingers together. "Let's get started."

Emmett walked away from her and sat next to Beau.

"Isn't she amazing?" Beau murmured.

"Yeah, she is," Emmett returned.

Cambree kept her eyes facing forward, but her cheeks were burning and her stomach was swirling. Emmett and Avalyn. It made so much sense. Cambree couldn't help but look down at her sweat-stained tank top and workout shorts. She had not a smidgeon of makeup on, and though she'd applied her clinical-strength antiperspirant and extra body spray this morning, she'd worked out too hard to not stink like sweat. The disparity between her and Avalyn Shaman was so glaringly obvious. Avalyn glowed with confidence and poise. *That* was the type of woman who should be on a Hawk brother's arm. It was humiliating that Cambree had ever imagined she could have a chance with someone like Emmett Hawk. The vision standing in front of their small group was the perfect complement to Emmett.

Avalyn was talking excitedly about goals and motivators and

the keys to success. The words whirled around Cambree's head, not really sinking in at all. She pretended to take notes on the pad of paper in front of her. Maybe someday the words would help her, but right now it was a way to distract her from looking at Emmett. If he caught a glimpse of her eyes, he'd see that she was acting like a green-eyed monster, and she was terrified for what Avalyn's appearance here meant to their fledgling relationship. No, they didn't even have a relationship. She bit at her lip to keep from crying out and scribbled away on the pad of paper, hating that her pen scratches swirled before her eyes as tears of frustration stung her eyelids.

Emmett enjoyed listening to Ava speak, as always. She'd been his friend since they were small children, and he was proud of all she'd accomplished. It was great of her to come and share with their small group her insights on goals and motivation, and it was fun to see how excited Gunner, Lucy, and his trainers were. Britney listened intently but seemed a little standoffish. She kept glancing at Cambree. Cambree was taking notes ... diligently. He couldn't catch her eye, but he'd be able to chat with her soon.

After the speech, he walked Ava out to her car, thanked her, gave her a big hug, and told her he'd see her soon. He hurried back inside to find Cambree. She was sitting in the same spot, but glanced up as he approached her.

"Hey," he said, leaning against a table. "Wasn't Ava great?"

"Yeah. She's amazing." Cambree bent to write some more.

"I can have her email you the notes," he suggested.

"Thanks, that would help so much." Cambree stood. "You two are close."

"Oh, yeah. Our whole lives we've been close."

Cambree pulled in a breath and then muttered, "That's ... great. You ready to go?"

"Sure."

She hurried in front of him, then stopped abruptly outside. "Where to first?"

Emmett stared at her. She usually followed that question up with "bossy man." Had he said something wrong? "Well, let's lift first, and then we'll focus on obstacles."

"Okay." She practically ran for the gym.

Emmett followed more slowly, confused and a little frustrated. He'd been so excited with his surprise of Ava coming here and had gotten really stoked to talk all her points through with Cambree, but Cambree was acting really weird. Maybe she was just upset that their time together was dwindling, but they'd keep seeing each other. He wasn't going to let someone as unreal as Cambree out of his life.

CHAPTER NINE

The afternoon had passed awkwardly for Cambree. Emmett kept saying things about how great "Ava" was and wanting to chat about different points she'd brought up. Cambree tried to agree and discuss enthusiastically. She didn't want Emmett to see her jealousy, but she had no clue how he was oblivious to it.

Their time together was almost over. Cambree wished she could stay in this week forever, but that was silly. Emmett would go on with his ritzy life. He'd find happiness with Avalyn, or someone like her, and Cambree would pray she could someday forget his kindness, his teasing, his kisses. It wasn't going to be easy, but that was life.

After dinner, she and Britney were headed toward the swimming pool together. Britney had shown up for their morning run with no makeup on, and Cambree had noticed she'd pushed herself harder than ever today and cheered everyone else on.

"I'm super proud of you," Cambree said.

"Thanks, friend. I'm proud of myself." Britney grinned. They walked into the pool area, the first ones to arrive. "What do you say we cheat and soak in the hot tub first?"

"I'd love that."

They shed their cover-ups and flip-flops and slid into the warm water. Of course, it reminded Cambree of kissing Emmett in this bubbly water and touching his beautifully formed chest. Why did "never again" have to hurt so much?

"So, 'my friend, Emmett Hawk,' huh?"

Cambree sighed. She wished she and Emmett Hawk had something together, but it could never be. "He's one of the best guys I've ever known." And soon that's how she'd remember him.

"He is a great guy." Britney smiled, but then she turned serious. "I don't know how to say this, but ... I saw him walk Avalyn out."

Cambree felt a stirring of unease in her gut. She leaned closer. "Are they together, Brit?"

Britney shrugged her lean shoulders. "Ah, sweetie." She pushed water around with her hands. "It sure seems like it."

"I want to go Google them, but I haven't let myself."

"They've been photographed together a lot and he supports her charities," Britney said quietly.

Gunner and Beau walked into the pool area, but they were still far enough away they wouldn't overhear them. Gunner raised his hand and called out, "Hey, pretty ladies."

They both waved.

"The thing is, Brit ... Didn't they look perfect together?"

Britney stared at her. "Do you love him?" she demanded to know.

Love. What a word. Cambree had loved once, and it had devastated her. Why was she destined to love men who didn't fit her? "I hardly know him."

"But you two get along so well." Britney sighed and then said, "You told me that you were uncomfortable with high society. Is that a serious issue, or something you can get over?"

Cambree pulled in a breath. The way Nolan had shredded her confidence and her heart wouldn't easily be erased. "It's pretty serious."

Britney eyed her compassionately. "Have you seen Emmett's family? The great Hawk brothers?"

Cambree knew exactly what Britney was talking about. "I have Googled them."

Britney nodded. She'd proven her point. "I hope you can get over your issues. You two really are great together."

No, he and Avalyn were great together. Emmett and Cambree were not a match and never would be. Even if Emmett wanted to date Cambree outside of this camp, she couldn't simply "get over her issues" when *she* was the issue. Nolan had destroyed her, but he hadn't been wrong. She was bluntly honest and had never learned social skills, and her mama was twenty times worse. Cambree didn't want to hurt Emmett or his family, even if it was unintentional like the way she'd messed up Nolan's job opportunity before he dumped her.

Emmett and then Mark, Tracy, and Lucy walked into the pool area. Cambree's stomach swooped with anticipation and excitement when she saw Emmett, but then it dropped like a tractor driven off a silo. She wasn't right for him, no matter how amazing he was and how she'd felt when they kissed.

"Hey!" Gunner yelled at Emmett. "Hit me!" He tossed a football to Emmett, then took a stance on the diving board.

Emmett grinned. "Let's see how far you can jump." His eyes sought out Cambree, and his grin grew.

Cambree returned his smile, but the worry she'd had about fitting into his high-dollar life hit her full force. Britney hadn't asked in order to make her uncomfortable; she was honestly concerned about her. Cambree was concerned, too. It seemed this carefree, happy time was going to end faster than she'd even dreaded.

Emmett had looked forward to a night of kissing Cambree in the hot tub or out on a walk through the woods—really, he didn't care about the location as long as she was in his arms. But she was stiff and awkward with him throughout the swimming time. After it was over she slipped away with Britney, and he ended up chatting with Gunner about recruiting and what to expect. When he finished, he hurried to his cabin to shower, then went to knock on Cambree's door.

She swung the door open and smiled, but there was something in her eyes that he didn't like.

"Walk?" he asked.

"Can you come in?" she asked at the same time.

"Sure." If she wanted to kiss and/or snuggle on the couch, he was all in.

They sat side by side on the couch. He scooted closer so their bodies were pressed against each other. She turned and brought her knees up underneath her, creating some distance between them. Emmett wanted to curse. What was happening?

"So, um, I like you ... a lot," she said.

Emmett forgot all about wanting to curse. She liked him, a lot. Yes! Of course his bold, too-honest Cambree would be the first one to initiate relationship talk. He was smitten with her.

He tried to move closer, but her knees were in the way. He gave up on the scooting and simply wrapped his arms around her waist and lifted her onto his lap. Ah, much better. "I like you a lot too." He leaned close, ready to seal all this "like" between them with lots and lots of kissing.

Cambree gave him one delicious taste of her lips, but then she shook her head free and pushed against his chest. "Emmett ... no."

He blinked, not sure what was "no." There was nothing "no" about that kiss, unless she was interpreting it vastly different from what he'd intended. Why she was saying his name all stern like she was a schoolteacher or something? Wait, she *was* a schoolteacher. But he wasn't some naughty student. He was her boyfriend, or at least hoping to be.

Cambree scooted off of his lap and back onto her own couch cushion. Emmett's shoulders rounded. What had he done wrong? "What's going on, Cam?" He clenched one fist and tried to keep his face neutral.

She swallowed before saying, "A lot of your life is about image, social rank, looking the part."

He shrugged. "Yeah. Why?"

Cambree took in a long breath, then pushed it out. "That's not me, Emmett. I hate social posturing. I can't do it."

Emmett blinked at her. Did she think he'd expect her to be some society princess to date him? He didn't want a Barbie doll like Britney. He thought he'd made that pretty clear this week. "I don't care if you want to be a hermit. I still want to date you."

Admittedly, if things progressed beyond dating, she'd have to deal with some media scrutiny and some high-profile parties with his parents, but he'd be by her side through it all. It wasn't that hard.

She shook her head. "Think about it for a minute. It wouldn't work. The media's always after you, and not just because you're an NFL star. It's your family, your money, the way you look." She gestured to him. "It's your life. You're a Hawk brother."

She said that like it was a bad thing. He was proud to be a Hawk brother. His brothers were some of the best men he knew.

"I like you, Emmett, you're a great guy, but this can't go any farther. I'm not willing to put myself in the limelight for you."

Emmett couldn't do anything but stare at her. She didn't say any more. He stood, suddenly angry and hurt. So he was great, but not great enough for her to handle a little media heat, a couple of snooty parties? Really? "You're already in the limelight with your Warrior races."

She stood too. "Not really. We have a few fans, but it's nothing compared to your life. I can't be a part of your world. No interviews, no media coverage, no paparazzi following me, and especially no chance for me to say something I shouldn't." She shook her head. "I'm so sorry, Emmett."

He clamped his jaw shut. How could the bravest woman he'd ever met not be brave enough to deal with the limelight, with society and paparazzi? It didn't fit. "So you won't be a victim and you'll stand up to sleaze balls like Troy, you're braver and tougher than anyone I know, but you won't stand up to the media for me?" So it was him. He wasn't enough for her.

"I wish I could explain it."

"Try."

Cambree looked him over. Then she glanced down and said quietly, "I was engaged not that long ago."

Emmett's stomach tumbled at the thought of her in another man's arms.

"I loved him, would've done anything for him, and he claimed he was crazy about me, didn't care about my background or the way I phrase things sometimes." Her shoulders rounded. "But I screwed it all up, really bad. I humiliated him and the governor and the governor's wife. I ruined his hopes to be appointed to the governor's staff. He dumped me and broke my heart. I can't walk on eggshells all the time, terrified that one wrong word will ruin the life of someone I ... care for. I can't live like that."

Emmett stared down at her. "He was an idiot, Cambree. I would protect you from situations like that. I wouldn't put you in situations you didn't want to be in."

She lifted her shoulders but didn't give him an inch. "You couldn't protect me from every situation. I want to stand on my own, Emmett, and I don't want to be scrutinized for being a redneck if I say something your type of people would say is wrong."

"You don't even *know* my type of people. You're judging me and my family off of some idiot who dumped you because you said something wrong?"

"I say things wrong all the time."

"You're brutally honest, but I love that about you." He wished he would've had time to let Ava and Cambree get to know each other today. Then Cambree would've understood that one of his closest friends was amazing and in the limelight, but she didn't care about "social posturing," as Cambree called it; she cared about helping others, especially children.

"I'm sure your family are great people, but will all your fans, sponsors, and family like the way I talk? My background?"

"I don't care if they don't." Why was she being so pigheaded about this? He was a grown man and could choose who he dated.

"You should. Your life is important to you."

"My family is important to me, but they would love you." Emmett shoved a hand through his hair. So his dad and Callum might struggle with where she'd come from and some of the ways she phrased things, but they'd learn to love her quickly. "You're right that the media is tough and being in the limelight sucks. I understand. Believe me, I do. My agent is forcing me to keep my early retirement under wraps and I hate that I'm basically lying to America, but you do what you have to do to keep everybody happy ..." His voice trailed off at the way her blue eyes darkened.

Half a second passed as she blinked up at him, then finally said, "You're retiring?"

Emmett clamped his lips together. He liked Cambree more than he should, but she was basically dumping him right now and he was spilling all his secrets. "We're waiting to announce it."

"Is that what *you* want?"

"No, but I have no choice." He pointed to his knee angrily. Why would he want to give up the sport he'd loved since the day he started playing catch in the backyard with Creed? "I'll never be back to a hundred percent."

Cambree blinked up at him. "That's not the Emmett Hawk that I know. The Emmett Hawk that I know would fight until he was even stronger than before."

Emmett didn't like the veer in the conversation, and it ticked him off that she thought she knew him, yet she didn't know or trust him well enough to know he didn't care about social status and that he'd never dump her if she said something wrong. "It is what it is."

"I thought the Hawk brothers never quit."

Emmett rubbed at his neck, which was burning hot. "I have no choice, Cambree, and you have no clue how hard it is."

She simply stared at him. "Exactly. It's hard because you have to keep up appearances, right?"

He couldn't deny it.

"It's too much, Emmett. You had to hide the truth about not being able to play again because you're worried about your image. You're a Hawk, and you all have to be perfect." Cambree shook her head. "This just confirms exactly what I'm trying to explain. I won't live like that."

The silence between them was heavy and thick. Emmett felt like she was disappointed in him or something, but that wasn't fair. She didn't understand the pressure of the media and keeping up his family image. Well, maybe she did. Cold dread washed over him as he realized this was exactly what she was saying to him.

Finally, Cambree spoke again. "Like I said, I really like you, but we're just too different, definitely not a fit. It's just smarter to end it now before we get involved and somebody gets hurt. I'm sorry."

Emmett didn't think that deserved a response. His heart was already involved, but he would never pressure her. If this was truly the way she felt, he was out. He strode from her cabin and into the warm night air. Breaking into a jog, he headed for the lake. After a few days of heaven with an incredible woman who was better than anything he'd ever dreamed of, he was slammed back to reality. He guessed maybe she was right—it was better now than later—but even if they'd dated for years, he couldn't imagine it could hurt any worse than this.

CHAPTER TEN

The next day was excruciatingly long yet too fast. Cambree wanted to savor each moment with Emmett before she said goodbye, but he was closed off and not himself, so the moments weren't really that great. Not that she blamed him—she'd made the choice to not pursue a relationship with him, and she hadn't even told him the whole of it, that she'd Googled all the pictures of him and Avalyn together. They fit so perfectly. She should've questioned him about their relationship, but it was easier to blame it on her unwillingness to be part of his wealthy crowd, which was also true.

If only he could understand how shattered she'd been after Nolan. Nolan had treated her like gold, elevating her from a life of hard work and making her feel like a princess. She thought she'd found the love of her life, and then, when she asked if the governor's young wife was expecting at a state dinner—which she obviously was—Cambree became the jerk that everyone wanted to hate.

Nolan had escorted her from the dinner and explained her faux pas—the governor was already humiliated about being a fifty-year-old father who'd had an affair with a much younger woman, then divorced his older wife and married the new girl quickly. Everyone was expected to not talk about it, as the press were already going to slay him enough. Then Nolan got the text that he was off the governor's staff because of Cambree. It had devastated him. He'd explained that she wasn't cut out for his life, told her she was trailer trash and that he never should've given her a chance no matter how beautiful she was, and asked for the engagement ring back.

Before that night, Nolan had been nothing but attentive and loving to her, always laughing at her little quips and her honesty, telling her how refreshing and unique she was. To imagine Emmett telling her she wasn't good enough for his life like Nolan had done made her heart twist painfully. Besides, Emmett already had someone who would be perfect for him—Avalyn.

The camp was officially over after dinner. Cambree had showered after an intense day of training, Emmett barking out commands like a drill sergeant; she'd just obeyed, not calling him "bossy man" once. He was also very careful not to touch her or even look at her, though she'd caught him glancing at her a few times before he averted his gaze. She hated that she was hurting him, but he'd realize soon that it was for the best. They were just raised too differently and had too different of lives and goals to try a relationship, even if there was no perfect Avalyn for him to be with.

Cambree put on a sleeveless summer dress, heels, and makeup for the first time this week. She hoped Emmett would notice, but she wasn't being fair. She was being the Nolan and ruling him out of her life, but he would understand one day that it was easier now before they fell any deeper for each other. If only it didn't hurt so much.

When she walked into the dining area, Emmett glanced up and she could see his chest expand as he pulled in a breath. He gave her a tentative smile. She started walking his way, but then Gunner grabbed her arm. "Wow! You clean up nice, pretty lady."

Cambree laughed. She wanted to sit by Emmett, but it was better not to fall any deeper for him. It was for the best, but the pain in her chest kept growing and growing.

Emmett's breath was knocked out of his body when he saw Cambree in a white sundress that showed off her tan, muscular shoulders, her dark hair falling long and loose down her back, and pink lipstick highlighting her perfect lips. He loved her. It hit him so hard. It had nothing to do with how gorgeous she was and everything to do with how amazing, tough, and genuine she was. Yet she didn't want him.

Gunner grabbed Cambree's arm and Britney slipped into the seat next to Emmett. The dinner passed miserably as Gunner flirted with Cambree and Emmett tried to endure Britney. She was a nice girl; she just wasn't Cambree. At least Lucy made it fun and kept them all laughing.

They finished with a delicious chocolate cake. "Finally! You let me have sugar after this miserable week." Lucy smacked her lips together and sighed. "Delicious."

Emmett thought Cambree was much more delicious than any dessert, but he couldn't have her, so he ate a big bite of the cake and agreed with Lucy that it was good.

"So Cambree's off to win her next Warrior race in her hometown," Lucy said, and everyone cheered. Emmett couldn't help but catch Cambree's eye. She gave him a shy smile and tucked a long curl behind her ear. Would she want him to come watch her race? No. If the media caught wind of him there, she wouldn't like it. He needed to wrap his fat head around what she'd made clear last night—she didn't want his lifestyle, or him.

When the dinner finally ended, Emmett walked outside and waited out front as the van pulled around. The staff loaded bags as the four participants told him and the trainers goodbye.

Britney gave him a quick hug. "This has been fabulous. Thank you."

"Thanks." Emmett was surprised she wasn't trying to hit on him or anything.

She climbed in and Gunner pumped his hand, slapping him on the back. "I feel ready to take on the season. Hope I see you on the field in a year, man."

Emmett pasted on a smile. He'd actually been able to put the pain of not playing this season to the back of his mind being busy with camp and especially falling for Cambree. Now he had nothing—no Cambree and no football. "Good luck," he said to Gunner. "I'll be cheering for you."

Gunner gave him a grin and climbed in.

Cambree was next. He shouldn't have done it, but he opened his arms and she snuggled up against his chest. Emmett's breath rushed out of him, and he wrapped her up tight and simply held her. It was so right, so perfect. How could she walk away from this? How could he let her?

She pulled back, and he forced himself to let her go. Blinking up at him, her blue eyes were bright. "Thank you, Emmett Hawk. I wish you a happier life than anybody deserves."

Emmett shook his head. She couldn't wish him away. If she'd only give him a chance. "Cambree, please."

She shook her head and backed against the van. "Bye," she whispered.

Emmett wondered if he'd imagined the catch in her voice and the tear rolling past her thick lashes.

Lucy tugged at him, and he followed, even though all he wanted to do was throw Cambree over his shoulder and run away with her. When he and Lucy were a little distance away from the van, she put both her hands on his cheeks and shook him. "What in the Sam Hill are you doing?"

"She doesn't want me," he choked out, looking at the van and unfortunately able to see Cambree through the large windows.

"Don't you be a dumby, boy. I love you two together. If she needs some space, I guess you gotta give it to her. I've seen magic before, but not quite like you two have." She gave him a motherly hug, then stepped back and patted his cheek. "Don't you give up."

Emmett couldn't give her anything.

She pushed out a sigh. "I'll be praying for you, honey child."

"Thanks," he muttered. Prayer was about the only hope he had now.

Mark escorted Lucy into the van and shut the door. Emmett stood, watching Cambree's beautiful profile in the window. As the van pulled away, she suddenly turned and looked at him, her blue eyes bright. The air whooshed from his lungs and he wanted to run after the van, holler for her to stay. She didn't do anything but stare at him, though, and he didn't do anything but stand there like an idiot, watching the most perfect woman he'd ever met be whisked away.

CHAPTER ELEVEN

Emmett was working with a youth group, fourteen- to sixteen-year-old football players, keeping himself busy and almost not moping every night for Cambree. He'd watched her in a race in California that he found online, and she did extremely well. She must've decided to do an extra race before the one in Breckenridge. She got second in the elite class. Her face at the finish line was happy but still determined. He could tell she wanted that number one. He wondered if she was keeping up on her training, and if she ever thought of him.

Mark came running into the weight room and yelled, "Emmett!"

Emmett blinked in surprise. Mark never got overly excited about anything.

"Your mom needs you."

"My mom?" Why hadn't she called his cell? He pulled it out and saw she had called, nine times. He turned his ringer off during camp, but he hadn't even felt it vibrate. He took the phone Mark extended to him.

"You should take it outside," Mark said.

Emmett's gut filled with dread. He nodded and mumbled "excuse me" to the young athletes. Mark instructed them to come with him. He'd combine them with his group of four and he'd be fine.

Emmett walked into the vacant hallway. He lifted the phone to his ear. "Mom?"

A wail like nothing he'd ever heard came through the line. There was so much pain in that scream that Emmett's hair stood on end. He wanted to sprint home and hold her.

"Emmett!"

"Mom?" His heart raced and his palms started sweating. "What's wrong?"

"C-creed," she managed to choke out.

Emmett leaned against the wall and slowly felt himself slide to the floor. He pulled his knees into his chest like a little child. "Please, no," he muttered.

"Come ... home," his mom begged.

Emmett nodded, though she couldn't see him. He couldn't form words right now. Creed was gone. His brother. His best friend. Gone.

He looked up to see Tracy standing there, watching him like he was unstable. "I'm coming," he finally managed to say.

"Love you," Mom said. "I love you so much." Then she was crying too hard to say more.

Tears pricked at Emmett's eyes. Oh, his mom. How she loved her boys. How would she survive without Creed? How would any of them? "I love you too."

Tracy stared at him as he struggled to stand. “What can I do?”

“Book me a flight home,” he muttered, banging through the exterior door and hoping he could drive himself to the airport without endangering anyone around him. Ah, Creed. Emmett had always thought if Creed died he'd know somehow, but he'd had no premonition. His heart screamed in pain and he heard himself cry out, “Creed!”

He sank to the ground next to his Lexus sport utility, sobbing out his anguish and muttering a prayer for his mom. How could his brother really be gone?

CHAPTER TWELVE

Emmett, his brothers, and his dad took turns letting his mom cling to them throughout the next week. Their mansion in the Hamptons felt too big and too quiet without Creed and his smart-aleck mouth around. Even Bridger was subdued, and though they had lots of friends and family stop by, everyone was awkward and sad. Even Bridger's brain-dead, usually hilarious friends were somber. Emmett hated it.

Late one night, his mom had finally cried herself to sleep again, and Emmett wandered out back by the pool, through the gardens, and down toward the waterfront. When he used to live at home, the rolling waves relaxed him. Now they made him think of Creed, the Navy SEAL who had grown up in the water and hardly ever wanted to leave it. The Navy hadn't disclosed any details of his death. There had been no bodies recovered. Had he drowned? Been shot? Tortured? Emmett passed a hand over his face, hating the questions, hating the hole in his heart that would never heal, hating to watch his mom's heart being shredded before his eyes.

"Hey, man." Bridger strode up the path from the beach and stopped in front of him. "Want to walk?"

Emmett didn't want to do much of anything, but he nodded and fell into step beside his brother. "How long you staying around?" Emmett asked as they meandered along the sand. It was beautiful with a half moon sparkling against the water. He loved where they'd grown up. The brothers were each two years apart and spent a lot of time together, but Emmett was having a hard time being here without Creed.

"I can't handle it much longer, you know? Mom sobbing. Dad all nice. Even Callum gave me a hug today." Bridger shuddered. "I hate it. I hate our family not being our family. I'm ready to go jump off a cliff in a wingsuit. Did you hear about the guy who jumped out of an airplane onto a net? No chute. That sounds like it would help me cope. But I can't even stand the thought of Mom losing another son."

Emmett completely agreed. He didn't want to say it, knew Bridger would hate it, but it came out anyway. "Be careful, bro. I'm already afraid she's never going to recover. If she lost you too ..."

"I know, but it's what I am. I'm an adventurer." He pushed out a breath. "Don't worry, I'll be careful. The wakeboarding gig has been fun and the death ratio's really low." He smiled, then grimaced. "Sorry."

"It's you, buddy. It's okay." Emmett was reminded of someone else who was too honest. He wondered what Cambree was up to, wondered if she knew about Creed. He wished they were close enough, or she cared enough, to come to him.

"Thanks. I'll stay through the memorial or whatever they're

doing. Poor Mom. No body to bury, no clue how he died. The Navy really sucks, you know that?"

Emmett laughed bitterly. "Yeah, they do."

Bridger glanced at him. "So what's your deal? You quitting the NFL?"

Emmett shrugged. "I guess. Knee won't ever be what it should be."

"Bull crap. I was being a jerk and trying to rile you. My brother is *not* a quitter."

Emmett stiffened. "I don't have a choice, Bridge."

"Um, yeah, you do. You're the toughest guy I know. Well, next to Creed, but ..." He shook his head. "Pull on your jockstrap and get to work, you loser."

Emmett stopped walking and Bridger stopped and faced him. "Lay off, dude. I ruined my knee, all right? I'm not quitting. I'm being smart about my future. Maybe you should smarten up, then grow up and stop taking chances."

Bridger's face tightened, he growled, and he launched himself at Emmett. Emmett should've known it was coming, but he'd been all soft and sad about Creed and hadn't had a brother attempt to take him out for a while. He slammed onto the soft sand on his back with Bridger on top of him. Bridger pushed his hands into his shoulders and yelled, "Fight me, you quitter!"

"No," Emmett said. Bridger didn't deserve the punch in the face that Emmett should give him.

"We are Hawks!" Bridger yelled in his face. "Creed would never give up. I don't know how he died, but I know he died fighting. You get off your butt and fight, or I'll beat you until you do."

Emmett actually laughed, though thinking of Creed fighting to his death made him want to curl in a ball. "You could never beat me, you brain-dead adrenaline junkie who doesn't care about anything but his next death-defying rush."

Bridger released one shoulder and slugged him in the face. Emmett roared and bucked his body, throwing Bridger to the side. He rolled up and landed a hard punch against Bridger's chest. Bridger went nuts, swinging at him and hollering who knew what. Emmett couldn't hear through the roaring in his head; he took more hits than he gave, and before too long they both had future bruises, black eyes, bloody noses, and blood dripping from cuts and scrapes. It was awesome.

"Yes!" Bridger screamed. "Yes, my brother's back!" He grabbed Emmett in a bear hug and they rolled around in the sand. When they stopped, Bridger squeezed him so tight. "You're such a jerk, and I totally love you, bro."

Emmett wiped away blood from a cut on his cheek and then pressed his hand to his nose to try to stem the flow. "You're a loser, and I couldn't love you more."

"I'm the loser?" Bridger sprung to his feet and offered him a hand up. Emmett took it and faced his little brother—"little" being a relative term. Bridger was fit and almost as big as Emmett. "Did your wee knee hurt while we wrastled?"

Emmett thought back to a few seconds ago, and with surprise, he said, "No."

"Are you ready to get your butt off the couch and start training? I'll push you back into fighting shape. It'll give me something to do instead of sit around and be sad."

Emmett considered it. What would it hurt to try? He had nothing without Cambree and Creed. Why not fight to play the game he loved?

"Come on, Creed's watching down from heaven and he's pissed off at you right now."

Cambree had said "pissed" too, and it had made Emmett smile. His stomach churned. If she'd only given his family a chance, she'd see they weren't a bunch of stuck-up snobs. He wondered what she was doing, if she ever thought of him. Though Cambree didn't want him, she had believed in him, and her example of pushing herself to the limit made him want to try as much as Bridger's challenging words.

"Creed's going to haunt me, eh?"

"Yes!" Bridger smacked him in the shoulder. "Come on, bro. For *me*." Bridger made his eyes big and pleading.

Emmett chuckled.

"I'm going to be on the front row at your first NFL game. First week in September, right?"

Emmett felt a smile grow on his face. His family's support had always meant the world to him. "Team starts practice next week."

"Are they going to kick you out if you show up?"

"I don't know that I have my position, but they'll give me a chance."

"Yes! Let's get training, bro." Bridger slapped him on the back. "Creed's gonna be bragging about you to his angel buddies."

"Thanks, man." Emmett sniffled, surprised there was any emotion left in him. He'd liked fighting Bridger a lot better than crying all week, and he loved that with Bridger he would now have a purpose: getting himself back into competition shape.

"So tell me about the girl, too," Bridger instructed as they walked back toward the house.

"What do you know about my girl?" Emmett challenged. His girl. Cambree didn't want to be his girl. That hurt much worse than his bloody nose and knuckles.

"Ava Baby might've slipped something when we were Snapchatting."

"I didn't even tell her about Cambree." He searched his memory, realizing with a start that he hadn't even introduced the two personally. He'd wanted to date Cambree seriously, but he hadn't introduced her to his close friend. That wasn't very classy of him.

"She said you couldn't keep your eyes off this gorgeous brunette, and the looks you two snuck at each other while she did her motivational speech were 'adorable.'" Bridger sighed and made a moony face.

"What does Ava know? She's only a psychiatrist."

Bridger chuckled. "She's pretty clueless about human interaction."

Emmett thought of Cambree that day, remembering how she took notes furiously and refused to meet his gaze. "I didn't even introduce them. Cambree acted off with me after Ava came, and then that night she told me she couldn't hack my wealthy lifestyle."

Bridger stared at him. "Ah, you're killing me. How can we even be brothers?"

"What are you talking about?"

"You're completely clueless. Cambree probably thought you were with Ava."

"Why would she think that?"

"Dude! Have you ever Googled yourself and Ava? There are so many pictures of you two at events. They even did that spread of you two in *The Rising Star*, how you were supporting her charity and all. Half the world thinks you're a couple."

"No. I've made it very clear we're close family friends."

"You're an idiot. Ava is the most gorgeous and accomplished

woman on the planet, and you show up at dinners and events with her all the time. Always guiding her around with your hand on her back." Bridger's mouth tightened. "Then you brought her in to speak at your camp and probably walked around holding her hand and grinning like the innocent idiot you are."

Emmett didn't like being called an idiot, but he was starting to see the problem. He only thought of Ava as a friend, but did Cambree see it that way? Was all of her lame reasoning why they shouldn't date simply a bunch of excuses because she thought he was with Ava? If that was true, she probably thought he was such scum, kissing on her and dating Ava. Aw, man.

"Really? You *were* holding Ava's hand?" Bridger's voice was edgy, totally unlike himself.

"No." He tried to remember. He'd been too focused on Cambree. "But she had her hand linked through my arm, and then I probably had my hand on her back." When Bridger glowered at him, he held up his hands. "I keep it high on her back, to be a gentleman," he clarified. "She's like my sister, you know that."

Bridger rolled his eyes. "Only you would sister-zone Avalyn Shaman. Idiot."

Emmett pushed at his brother's chest. "Stop calling me an idiot. I messed it up, all right?" His eyes narrowed. "You seem to think Ava's so perfect. Why aren't you dating her?"

Bridger guffawed. "So out of my league it's not even on the table to discuss." Emmett opened his mouth to protest, but Bridger pushed at his shoulder. "So you going after the Warrior princess, or do I need to pummel you again?"

Emmett drew in a long breath. He wanted to chase after Cambree and see if Bridger's theory about her thinking he was with Ava was correct, but what if she just rejected him again?

"Let's concentrate on me getting my spot back with the Titans first."

"Ah, you are still such a wimp." Bridger pulled him into a headlock and rubbed his knuckles on his head. Emmett pulled free and shoved him. "Stop being a loser and go after the girl."

Emmett shook his head. "Playing in the NFL again will be easier."

"When did a Hawk ever choose easy?"

Emmett arched his eyebrows. Creed hadn't chosen easy. Callum worked harder than any person he knew. Bridger was a screwball, but he was successful and driven to be the best, excelling at one extreme sport before moving on to the next. Maybe his carefree, crazy brother had a little wisdom in him.

CHAPTER THIRTEEN

Cambree waited at the start line of the Breckenridge Warrior race. Her nerves were taut and she had to force herself to ignore the crowd. Her entire family, church group, students, and friends from school and the community were all here cheering her on. There were signs everywhere showing support of their local Warrior. The race hadn't even started and she heard her name being shouted time and again. It felt fabulous ... and it was a crap-load of pressure.

A lot of familiar competitors were here, including Shayna, who'd beaten her by ten seconds in California a couple of weeks ago. Cambree hated losing, even to someone as impressive as Shayna.

Cambree had already done the shaking hands, wishing everyone a great race, etc. Now it was time to put all the hard work of her week in Texas, and everything Emmett had taught her that she'd continued to implement since, into practice. This was her race; she could feel it. She was prepared, she was in the best health of her life, and even though he would never know it, she was racing this for Emmett and his family. She'd seen the news about his brother, Creed, being killed. Her heart had ached and she wanted to go to him, but she didn't truly know him that well, even though she thought she did, and it seemed trite and unfair of her to go chase him down because he'd had a horrible tragedy. It would still never work for them to be together, so she'd focused on her training and prayed for Emmett and his family, knowing she would win this race for him.

The gunshot went off and she sprinted out of the gate. She had an immediate lead and felt like she was flying. She could hear Emmett's voice in her head, almost as if he were right there beside her, pushing her to sprint harder, saying, "That's my girl!" She ignored the other competitors and took strength from the crowd cheering her on as she completed the barbed wire crawl, the slippery wall, the spear throw. She did have to stop and do thirty burpees, but they were a breeze and she smiled the whole time, thinking of Emmett. She continued through obstacle after obstacle and sprinted like she was being chased by a warthog between each one. The wall jumps and rope climb were easy. The big cargo net and Hercules hoist were a struggle, but before she knew it, she was sprinting toward the last obstacle and her name was being yelled so ferociously she forced herself to look around and notice where her competitors were. She had a clear lead.

"Yes!" she screamed out, moving even faster. She could see the final obstacle for this track—the eight-foot wall. Her stomach dropped. She had to get over it quickly, or the other racers would catch up. Memories of trying to scale this wall at the fitness camp and failing after being attacked by Troy raced through her mind. She forced them away and focused her thoughts on Emmett. Even though he wasn't here, he had believed in her. She could do this.

She swiped her sweaty palms across her shorts as she ran. It didn't help much, as she was dirty and wet. Her heart threatened to burst out of her chest as she leapt, planted her knee into the wall, and thrust herself up with the momentum. She clasped her right hand on the top of the wall. Her hand started to slip, but she gritted her teeth and held on. Her arm felt like it was going to rip out of the socket, but she ignored it and propelled her body upward, grasping with her left hand. She flipped her body over the top of the wall and dropped to the other side.

Cambree heard a horribly loud pop and her left knee gave out. She dropped into the dirt. The crowd seemed to suck in air as one, and then cries of exclamation rang in her ears. Cambree knew she had the lead, but it was at least two hundred yards to that finish line. She forced herself to her feet and heard another pop as she straightened her leg. She started limping forward. Her knee hurt, but not horribly, and she put more pressure on it and pushed herself to run faster. The crowd was screaming, but she wasn't certain if it was cheers of encouragement or screams of concern and people urging her to stop.

Cambree tried to ignore it and she didn't let herself look over her shoulder, but she could feel her competitors gaining on her. She just wasn't moving fast enough.

Then she heard it: a deep, wonderful voice yelling, "Come on, sweetheart!"

Her eyes sought the voice, and right next to the finish line was the most exquisite face. She wanted to scream his name, but she focused all her energy on his encouraging voice instead, and she upped her speed.

"That's my girl! You're so tough! You've got this!" Emmett

was yelling so loud for her that it drowned out all the other voices. "Go! Go! Go!"

Her knee hurt, but that just made her think of Emmett even more. His knee hurt, yet he was still so tough. She was running this race for him and now he was here? It was craziness, but her heart threatened to burst out of her chest, she was running so fast and hard, and she completely ignored her knee and pushed herself into full sprinter mode.

"Yes!" Emmett hollered. "Go, sweetheart!"

Cambree flew across the finish line, breaking through the flimsy tape, and collapsed in the dirt. She could hear the crowd yelling and other racers thundering past her, but all she wanted was to find Emmett. She struggled to her feet, but strong arms wrapped around her and lifted her up.

Emmett cradled her close to his chest and grinned down at her. "You did it."

Cambree leaned into him, trying to catch her breath. "You're here," was all she could manage.

He bent down and brushed his lips over hers. "I wouldn't miss it."

She sighed with longing for him. She wanted to kiss him long and hard and never let him go. "I smell worse than a bag of moldy potatoes," she muttered, trying to push her sagging ponytail out of her face.

He chuckled. "Oh, Cam. I don't even know what that smells like."

"Spoiled rich kid." She smiled up at him. "I was racing for you."

"You were?" He leaned closer, seeming content to just hug her.

"That's Emmett Hawk!" Voices penetrated through their

bubble, and then there were phone cameras clicking and people all over them, asking what Emmett was doing here, asking if Cambree was okay, asking how she felt about her first win.

Emmett swept her completely off her feet and elbowed his way through the crowd. "Excuse me, we need to get Cambree checked out." He bent down closer to her. "Did you injure anything when you fell, sweetheart?"

"My knee."

He nodded and held her closer. She hated that she was so dirty and stinky, but she loved that he was here. He didn't seem to even notice how gross she was, but then again, he'd worked out with her for a week and had never complained.

Cambree hid her head in the firmness of his chest, not responding to the crowd around them. If she said something and it embarrassed Emmett and his family, after all they'd been through with losing Creed, she would never forgive herself.

Her mom and her sister, Jasmine, rushed into view. Cambree didn't have time to ask where the rest of the family was before her mom stared up at Emmett and demanded, "Who are you, and why do you have your big fat hands on my girl?"

Cambree tried to burrow right into Emmett's chest. He smelled so clean and manly, and if Cambree didn't embarrass him with the media, her mom and siblings surely would.

"I'm Emmett Hawk," he said as if they were meeting for coffee. "Sorry I can't shake hands right now, but I love your daughter and I want to get her to medical help."

"You love—?" Cambree was glad she wasn't standing up. The world swirled around her.

Emmett pressed his lips to her forehead as he continued plowing through the crowd with her mom and sister in tow. He got to a Range Rover and hurried around to the passenger side.

The door beeped at them, and Emmett slid her gently to her feet and eased the door open. "I wish you could stay to celebrate your win, but you need to get that knee checked out."

Cambree looked over his shoulder at her mom; her dark eyes were big and uncertain. "Wait a minute, Mister Ranger Rover," her mom said. "I don't trust pushy, handsome, bossy men with my daughter."

Emmett smiled. "She talks like you," he said to Cambree.

Cambree's cheeks flared. "She's a bit overprotective."

"Understandable. I'm a little overprotective of you too, love."

Cambree nodded, ready to pass out from being close to Emmett again, staring at his handsome face, feeling his perfect facial hair brush against her cheek, and the way he kept throwing the "love" word around.

Emmett looked to her mom and sister. "Would you like to ride with us, or meet us at the hospital?"

The crowd was pressing in around them and Cambree couldn't even count how many people had their phones up, recording the interaction.

"Cambree, do you trust this yahoo?" her mom demanded. "He's bigger than a Sasquatch, and he looks a little too uppity for my blood."

Cambree stared into his dark eyes. "Yes," she whispered. "I trust him."

Emmett grinned, lowered his head, and kissed her for the entire world to see. Cambree clung to his neck and pulled herself even closer to him as his arms tightened around her. His lips were firm and as perfect as she remembered. She savored his kiss, until she remembered there were phones recording everywhere. Pulling back, she met her mom's surprised gaze.

"All-righty, then." Her mom tsked, but there was a sparkle in her dark eyes. "We gotta get the rest of our herd. You be careful with my girl." She puffed out her chest as if she had a chance of shoving Emmett around.

Emmett nodded seriously. "I will." He settled Cambree into the vehicle and gave her one more soft kiss before shutting the door.

Cambree leaned back against the headrest, drained and in shock. Was this all some crazy dream? Emmett was here, she'd just won a Warrior race, and her knee was hurt. She looked down and saw that it was already swelling. Ah, crap. But she couldn't find the energy to be upset. Emmett was here.

She watched him push through the crowd pressing in on him outside the vehicle before he was able to open his door and slide inside. He clicked the lock button and turned to stare at her. "Wow, you're pretty."

Cambree let out a surprised laugh and ran her hand through her mud-caked hair. She glanced around at the pristine leather interior. "I'm like a pig fresh from the sty in your pristine car."

He chuckled. "It's a rental." He pushed the start button, but reached over and wrapped his hand around hers instead of putting it into gear. "Do you have any clue how much I've missed you?"

She held up her other hand and held her thumb and first finger an inch apart. "A little?"

"No. Horribly. I've ached for you."

Cambree wanted to tell him that his ache was over, but nothing had really changed with their relationship since they'd seen each other. She'd ached for him too and he'd lost his brother, but her fears of the media blasting her and her family, and all of them embarrassing him and his family, were worse than ever. The way her mom had talked to him with everyone videoing? Her face flamed just thinking about it.

Emmett pulled a small drink cooler from the back seat and set it in her lap. “I hoped I might get to see you after, so I brought you some recovery fuel.”

Cambree undid the zipper and pulled out a chocolate muscle milk. There was fruit, protein bars, water, Gatorade, and even a Coke. She lifted the Coke out. Her chest warmed at his thoughtfulness.

Emmett shrugged. “Some people online said it helped with recovery.”

“Never tried it, but thanks.” She opened a water bottle and drained half of it, then popped the lid on the muscle milk and took a long swallow.

Emmett had this perma-grin on as he dropped the Range Rover into reverse and slowly backed up. The rearview camera was beeping as there were still people all over the vehicle, but the crowd gradually dispersed and let them through. She saw some of the race organizers pushing people away. Emmett made it away from the crowd and was able to flip around and get onto the road. Neither of them said much as she ate and drank and gave him directions to the hospital.

Emmett parked in the emergency room circle drive, opened his door, and jogged around to open hers.

“You can’t park here,” someone said.

“My girlfriend needs help,” Emmett told them.

Girlfriend? Oh, how she wished. She was still shocked that he was here, but he was acting exactly like she’d known he would: taking charge of the situation and just being his thoughtful, amazing self.

Emmett bent down and lifted her into his arms.

"I think I could hobble," she said. "I did just sprint to the finish line."

"Don't take all my fun away," he said.

"Smelling my sweaty, muddy body is fun?" She wrinkled her nose.

"You're perfect all the time, love."

Cambree blushed at him calling her "love" again. How could she refute him, though? He was so perfect to her.

"You really can't park here."

Cambree looked up and saw a young guy in green scrubs.

"Sorry. The keys are in it if you need to move it." Emmett strode away from the guy.

"They'll tow you!" the guy hollered at Emmett's back.

"It's a rental," Emmett said.

Cambree laughed. "Does anything ever tick you off?" she asked.

Emmett paused outside the doors and glanced down at her. "Being without you," he said softly.

"What made you come?" she had to ask.

"Creed died." The pain was stark in his eyes, and Cambree wanted to comfort him so badly. "My family's a mess, but Bridger tried to thrash me. I won, of course. And he told me Creed would be ticked at me for not trying. He meant the NFL, but then we talked about you and ..." He shook his head. "I'm gonna play this year, somehow. Practice has been going amazing, but being with you is more important to me than that."

Cambree's eyes widened. "You hardly know me, Emmett."

"I know enough to know I want to be with you." His eyes were begging her now.

Cambree couldn't commit to anything. She'd just finished a physically and emotionally exhausting race. His brother had recently died. Their interaction after the race was going to be all over the internet and would probably humiliate him and his family, and she still hadn't asked him about his relationship with Avalyn Shaman.

"Don't say anything," he said. "Let's figure out your knee and we can talk later."

Cambree appreciated the out. "Okay."

They walked through the sliding glass doors and approached the nurse's station. The nurse's eyes widened as they drew closer. "You're Emmett Hawk and Cambree Kinley."

Cambree frowned. She didn't know this girl from high school or anything.

"I've been watching the video from the Warrior race," the nurse gushed. "How you kept going after you fell, and then Emmett Hawk lifting you into his arms and kissing you. Ah," she sighed. Then she grinned. "Your mom called Emmett Hawk a 'big yahoo' and a 'Sasquatch.'" She giggled. "They keep replaying that on clips."

Cambree pushed out a breath. Emmett held her tighter. "Can we get her in with an orthopedic specialist as soon as possible?" he asked.

"Oh, of course. Take a seat and I'll find out who's on call." She winked and gave them a thumbs-up as she picked up the phone.

Emmett walked over to the chairs lining the walls. Luckily there were only a couple of people in the waiting room, although those people were staring at them. He settled into a chair with her in his arms.

Cambree tried to move out of his arms, but he held her fast. "Please, Cam. Let me hold you."

She relaxed into him, realizing she just wanted him to hold

her also. There was no way to wrap her mind around him staying with her beyond today, so she wanted to enjoy every moment she got.

Emmett held on to Cambree as her family piled into the waiting room, and he tried to keep all of her siblings' names straight, loving the little guy, Luke, who obviously worshipped him. The nurses finally escorted them back to a room. Emmett wouldn't let Cambree go. She seemed like she wanted to be in his arms, but he had this awful feeling she wasn't going to stay here. Her mom had done exactly what she'd been worried about, made him look bad for the media. How did he explain that he didn't care? He always would've chosen Cambree over a good media presence, but losing Creed had just solidified his need to be with her. He hadn't smiled this much in weeks.

He, Cambree, and her mom had just gotten settled into a small room when a doctor rushed in. He reached out to Emmett and pumped his hand. "Charles Young. I'm a huge fan. Huge." The guy's grin was wide, like the Joker on *Batman*.

"Emmett Hawk." Emmett smiled, hoping this meant they would get help for Cambree quick.

Dr. Young shook his head. "It's such an honor. After I help Cambree, would you sign something for me?"

"Sure. Can you please ..." He gestured to Cambree.

"Hi, Cambree," the doctor said.

"Hi, Charles."

So they obviously knew each other.

"How did you meet Emmett Hawk?" the doctor asked.

"Just look at my knee, you dork," Cambree said, folding her arms across her chest.

"Okay." He pushed out a breath and looked at her swollen and mud-caked knee. "Can you clean this first please?" the doctor asked a nurse who had just walked into the room.

She grabbed some wipes and swiped gingerly at Cambree's knee. Cambree tensed but didn't complain.

"Emmett Hawk." The doctor leaned back in his swivel chair thing, and Emmett wondered if he'd tip over.

Emmett forced a smile. This guy was getting annoying. He wanted to know what was wrong with Cambree's knee, not deal with an obsessed fan.

"Charles, stop acting like a mental patient and fix Cambree," her mom demanded.

The doctor put up his hands. "Okay, okay."

Emmett hid a grin. He liked Cambree's mom.

The nurse finished quickly, and the doctor pushed Cambree's knee one way and another, messing around with her kneecap. He extended and flexed her leg, turning it one direction and another. Cambree grimaced.

"You heard a distinct pop when you hit the ground?"

"Yeah."

"Did you hear another pop when you stood?"

Cambree thought for a second, then said, "Yeah, I did."

"Let's do an MRI, but I'm ninety percent sure the sound was your kneecap popping out of alignment. But it most likely popped back in on its own when you straightened it. A subluxated patella. If I'm right, and I usually am—" He grinned cockily. "—you'll have some swelling and pain and you'll need to stay off of it for a few weeks, but you should make a quick and easy recovery with a little bit of physical therapy. Shall we do the MRI?"

"Yes," Cambree said. "Thanks, Charles."

He stood and went to wash his hands, then came straight back to Emmett. "Autograph?"

"Sure." Emmett laughed and signed the pad of paper Charles produced.

The doctor left with a promise to get Cambree into radiology quickly.

Cambree's shoulders relaxed as he left, and then she was sobbing. Emmett reached her first and hugged her tight to him. "You're okay," he said. He was so relieved. The thought of Cambree going through surgery and recovery for a knee had been weighing on him. It had been a painful and discouraging recovery.

"Okay, boy." Her mom shoved him. "You'd better move over and let the mama hold her girl, or I'll never give you my stamp of approval."

Emmett moved to the side but kept his arm around Cambree. "Can we share?" he asked.

Her mom laughed. "You've got grit, I'll give you that." She moved to Cambree's other side, and they both kept an arm around her.

Cambree didn't say much. Emmett was sure she was exhausted. He wished he knew where they'd go from here, what Cambree would want, or if she even wanted him, but he'd take it a step at a time and pray the good Lord and his brother Creed up in heaven would give him some help. Forget media presence and his family's pristine reputation. He couldn't lose Cambree again.

CHAPTER FOURTEEN

Cambree was settled in the recliner in her mama's living room. She'd wanted to go home to her own apartment, but her mama was having none of that. At least she'd been able to shower and put on Jasmine's tank top and shorts. Then Emmett had carefully rewrapped her knee.

It was wonderful to know her knee was all right after the MRI came back showing no damaged ligaments or tendons. She was content to be clean and relax into the chair, but she could have done without all of her siblings and her mama crowding into the small living area and staring at her and Emmett. He sat in a kitchen chair, pulled up close to her recliner, clinging to her hand. From his expression, she knew he wanted to talk to her alone.

When her siblings stopped asking questions about her knee and then grilling Emmett about football and the Titans and if he seriously loved their sister, which he answered yes to without any hesitation, her mama finally stood and clapped her hands together. "All right, you munchkins, outside to the park. These two need a minute." She winked at Emmett, patted him on the head, and said, "I approve."

Cambree closed her eyes. Of course her mom approved. Who wouldn't approve of Emmett? Why wasn't he the one running? Here they sat in her mama's single-wide trailer, with the whole crew grilling him and her mama being as blunt and crazy as ever. If the media caught sight of this circus, his poor family would get so much unwanted publicity that they would all hate her. Did they already hate her from what they'd probably seen today?

Her siblings were filing out when Isabel, the fifteen-year-old, pointed at the TV screen, which was always on, but thankfully it was at least muted today. "Look, Cam, you're the top story on *Entertainment News*."

Everyone froze, and somebody turned up the sound. The TV showed Cambree's fall, her run to the finish, and Emmett yelling encouragement to her. Cambree hadn't realized how close the next racer was behind her. She'd really won. She let that sink in, but then the reporter started talking about this Cinderella story. It felt like they were mocking her as they showed her mama trying to push Emmett around and Emmett looking so cute and manly as he carried Cambree, while Cambree was a muddy, disgusting mess.

Then the words she hated and dreaded came out: "From a humble life in a single-wide trailer to winner of a Warrior race and love interest of billionaire football star, Emmett Hawk. It would seem Cambree Kinley's luck is changing."

Her mama grabbed the remote and shut the television off.

That was a first. "Shoo. Go play." The teenagers mumbled about being too old to play, but she was not one to take any guff. She followed them out the door and shut it resolutely behind her.

Emmett turned to Cambree, still holding her hand. "Cam ... there's so much I want to tell you."

Cambree stared up at him. "Why aren't you running away?"

"Running away?" He blinked at her. "From what?"

"From me, from this!" She gestured angrily around the trailer. "My mama just humiliated you on national television. I grew up in this trailer, Emmett. You know what that announcer wanted to say: she wanted to call me trailer trash. I'm not worthy of you and your high-class-falutin' family."

Emmett came around and knelt in front of her. He took both of her hands in his and carefully avoided touching her knee. "Cam. I don't care about any of that."

Cambree wanted him to hold her. She wanted to kiss him. Yet she couldn't let this continue. "You should be with someone perfect."

"Like Avalyn?" The knowing look in his eyes hit her hard.

"Yes." She bit at her lip. "Are you with her?"

"No." He chuckled. "No, sweetheart. Ava's a close friend, but I don't love her. She's not right for me at all." He paused, and her heart raced at the smoldering look he bestowed upon her. "You are."

Cambree's heart soared. He didn't love Ava. He loved Cambree. But his love could easily cool and die like Nolan's had. "You say that now, Emmett. Someday soon you'll be embarrassed by me, by my family, my situation. Then you'll dump me like a hot rock." Tears leaked out, and she couldn't blame them on everything she'd gone through today.

Emmett shook his head. "Cam." He said her name so tenderly. "Sweetheart. I know you've been hurt. I know it's hard to trust, but don't shut me out."

Cambree couldn't promise anything, but she squeezed his hands.

"When I lost Creed ..." He looked down and blew out a breath. "I didn't know if I'd ever smile again. You've been there, right, with your dad?"

She nodded, and hot tears coursed down her cheeks—for Emmett, for his poor mom, for his family, and for herself and her mama and family. Nothing could heal the hurt, but life continued and eventually you smiled and laughed again, even though you felt guilty for it.

Emmett released one hand and rubbed the tears away from her cheek with his thumb.

"You and your big hands," she said.

Emmett chuckled. He rose up and kissed her cheek before lowering back onto his haunches. "This is what I'm talking about. I need this—I need *you*." He gazed at her with such love and pleading.

Cambree swallowed hard and then whispered, "I'm scared, Emmett."

"Me too, sweetheart. But if we don't take this chance, I'll never forgive myself. There's no happiness without you, Cam. You're my girl."

The possessive note in his voice made her stomach quiver. She wanted him so badly that she trembled. "Can we take it slow?" she asked.

Emmett whooped, stood, and scooped her out of the chair. He turned and settled into the chair with her in his lap, then proceeded to capture her lips with his. Thrills of pleasure raced through her mouth and coursed through her whole body. He pulled back and grinned. "I love you, Cam."

"There is nothing about your reaction and that phrase that are taking it slow." Yet she couldn't help but grin at him. She loved him too, but didn't know if she could verbalize it yet. Trust had to be earned, and it wouldn't be a speed race for her.

Emmett chuckled. "Sorry." He didn't sound repentant at all. "The thing that sucks—"

"You just said 'sucks,'" she interrupted him. "That sounds like me, not Mr. High-Class Billionaire."

"Sorry, the thing that *bites*—" He paused briefly when she giggled, then went on. "—is I have to get back for practice tomorrow, so can we start the taking it slow thing tomorrow? Unless you're ready to move to Dallas."

She placed her hands on his chest, reveling in the muscle underneath his shirt. "I'm not moving to Dallas anytime soon, but yes, we can wait for the taking it slow to start tomorrow."

"Yes!" He pulled her in tight and lowered his head close to hers. "You don't have to tell me you love me yet. I can see it in your eyes, though." He was so close that his breath tickled her mouth.

"Stop being so cocky, bossy man, and just kiss me already."

"Yes, ma'am," he drawled out in a fake but cute Texas accent. He kissed her and kissed her and kissed her. His lips were the perfect match to hers, and being his arms made her feel complete and yet more excited than a redneck at a demolition derby.

Cambree didn't worry about the pain in her knee, or the media disaster she knew was playing on phones and televisions everywhere, or the fact that she hadn't met his family and they might hate her. How could she worry while she was in Emmett Hawk's arms?

CHAPTER FIFTEEN

Cambree heard a rap on her condo door and her stomach filled with butterflies. Emmett was here. She ran to her bathroom and checked her reflection one more time. Her pale blue sundress set off her dark curls and made her eyes pop. She put on another layer of mint lip gloss and then hurried for the door. It had been almost two weeks and her knee was doing great. The swelling was gone, and though she wasn't cleared for Warrior races yet, she could move on it without any pain. But the best part of the last two weeks had been talking to Emmett daily and texting and Snapchatting even more often. She loved him, and though she was still terrified to meet his family, she would do it and try her best to not embarrass them, for Emmett.

Throwing the door wide, she grinned. "Em— Nolan?"

Nolan was dressed in his usual starched suit with his blond hair slicked back from his handsome face. His teal-colored eyes swept over her possessively. "Waiting for someone?"

Cambree folded her arms across her chest, partially because

her heart was threatening to pound out of her chest and partially because it would show him she couldn't be intimidated. "Yes, and you're not it. Get your keister off my property."

Nolan smirked. "Ah, Cambree. Always with the funny quips. I've missed you."

She rolled her eyes. "What do you want?"

"Another chance with you."

"Always with the funny quips. Please leave before my date shows up."

Nolan stepped closer. She could smell his spicy cologne. It was unpleasantly familiar, and the memories of Nolan and how low he'd made her feel made her stomach turn. He reached for her hand, but she pulled both her hands behind her and clenched them behind her back, so he settled for rubbing his palm down her bare arm. "You're absolutely beautiful."

"I'm not going to ask you again. Leave, or I'll have no choice but to use force." Her hands were trembling. She couldn't best Nolan in a fistfight, but she wasn't afraid of him like she had been of Troy. Nolan wouldn't hurt her physically, but he had devastated her emotionally. She couldn't let him get in her head.

Nolan chuckled, then spoke in a low murmur. "I know I broke your heart, but it was all a mistake. I understand you don't think you're worthy of me, but I love you and I'm willing to forgive your mis—"

She slugged him as hard as she could in the stomach. The breath whooshed out of him and he stumbled back from her door, hitting the exterior railing. "Wh—" he gasped out, holding his gut in surprise and pain.

"You did break my heart, but that was only because I was stupid and let you tear me down. I'll never let you make me think less of myself again. You're the one who isn't worthy of me." She pulled her fist back, ready to slug him again. "And if you don't leave, I'll hit you harder next time."

"Cam?" Emmett strode up to them, looking exquisitely perfect in a navy-blue suit with a red floral tie. "Everything okay?" He looked back and forth between her and Nolan, his dark eyes filled with concern.

"Emmett!" She ran to him and hugged him tight, clinging to the strong muscles in his back. He wrapped her up in his warm embrace, and all the angst of Nolan trying to drag her down evaporated in the safety of Emmett's arms.

"You have got to be kidding me," Nolan said. "You think Emmett Hawk or his family are going to put up with your redneck lingo once he gets what he wants from you?"

Cambree whirled from Emmett, ready to hit Nolan again. Emmett ushered her behind him and stormed toward Nolan.

Nolan's eyes widened and he backed away. "I'm sorry!"

"You're going to be sorry," Emmett growled.

Nolan ran faster than she'd thought possible, sprinting across the sidewalk and to the parking lot.

Emmett stopped and watched him go. "Do you want me to chase him and thump him?"

Cambree laughed. "No. I want you to kiss me."

Emmett grinned and strode back to her side. He framed her face with his hands and leaned down. His mouth met hers, and everything was truly right in her world. Cambree rose up onto tiptoes and clung to his biceps for support. The sheer strength and power of this man was awe-inspiring, but he was tender and perfect for her.

He pulled back and traced his thumbs along her cheeks. "Ah, Cam, I've missed you."

Then they kissed again, and she shut out everything but the pressure of his lips on hers.

When they came up for air, he was grinning. “You ready to go to dinner, love?”

Cambree drew in a breath and savored his warm, musky smell. “About that. What if we order in tonight?”

Emmett smiled, but then a worried expression crossed his face. “You don’t want to be seen with me in public yet?”

Cambree wanted to lie, but couldn’t. “It’s not that I don’t want to be seen with you. It’s just ... I don’t know if I’m ready to face the real world yet. Especially after ...” She claimed she was over Nolan’s emotional knockdown, but it was still hard to believe she was worthy of Emmett and could fit in with his family.

“You just stood up to that loser beautifully. You can handle anyone, love.” His dark eyes gleamed. “But I won’t complain if you want me all to yourself tonight.”

She wrapped her arms around his neck and squeezed him tight. “Thank you.”

“I do need a favor, though.”

“Anything.”

“Can you be at the opening game of the season in two weeks ... and sit with my family?”

Cambree blinked up at him, suddenly thinking that dinner out at a fancy restaurant with cameras clicking and paparazzi chasing them sounded much easier than facing the mighty Hawk family.

Emmett stared down at her, and he suddenly looked vulnerable and afraid. Cambree reminded herself that she had just stood up to Nolan. She drew in a breath. She was nervous she wouldn’t fit in with Emmett’s family, but she loved him and she trusted he wouldn't put her in a bad situation. If he wanted her there, she'd be there for him.

"I'll see if I can fit you in my schedule," she said.

Emmett whooped and kissed her. He swept her off her feet and carried her into her condo. "I'm thinking dessert first," he said.

"What's dessert, Hawk?" she asked.

"Your lips."

Cambree laughed, but he cut it off by slamming the door shut with his foot and lowering his mouth to claim hers. She'd never tasted any dessert so delicious.

CHAPTER SIXTEEN

It was the opening game of the season. Emmett hadn't been this nervous in his entire career. He'd worked so hard the past two months to be ready for this moment. His coaches and the team trainers claimed they were impressed, and he was starting in his position as the X receiver. He wasn't quite a hundred percent, but he would push through that missing five percent with sheer grit and cleverness, just like Cambree had done to win her race. He was playing for Creed today, and he would make his brother proud.

He swept his helmet off and glanced around as they lined up for "The Star-Spangled Banner." His teammates had a Navy trident on their helmets in support of Creed and the other five SEALs who had been killed. It touched something deep in Emmett's heart, their support, this brotherhood. He truly loved these guys like family.

The announcer told the crowd about Creed and his team's sacrifice for their country. Emmett focused on the flag as a young lady belted out the national anthem. Tears ran down his face, but he didn't brush them away. It was all tied up for him—his love of his brother, his love of Cambree, his love of his nation, his love of his family, and his love of his teammates and this game.

The national anthem finished and the Titans started shuffling around, getting ready for the kickoff and strapping helmets back on. The anticipation and energy on the sidelines before a game was indescribable. Emmett was so happy to be here.

Knox Sherman, the Beast, bumped Emmett's arm from the side. "Sorry about your brother, man."

Emmett had never heard the guy say that many words. He nodded. "Thanks."

"We're all proud to play for him." Then Knox turned and strode away, probably having exceeded his emotional or speech capacity. Emmett heard the guy had gotten married. He hoped his wife was a chatterbox.

Emmett smiled and turned to the stands. His parents were always on the front row, fifty-yard line. He spied his mom waving wildly at him, his dad lifting a stoic hand, then Callum imitating his dad. Bridger gave him a broad smile and the hang-loose sign—but where was Cambree?

She still absolutely hated the media exposure, and she and her mom had said some doozies that social media and even news outlets had their fun with, but he didn't care. Emmett had held a press release and told the media he was dating the toughest and most amazing woman in the world. There'd been all kinds of questions about their relationship and her background. He'd answered what he could and said "no comment" more times than he could count, and then he'd stayed as far away from the media as he could, practiced football, and talked to Cambree every chance he could get.

She was his light and his happiness. He didn't care if she said things bluntly. He loved it and always would. It had been hard for her to trust that he loved her, but he was slowly gaining that trust. Today was the day she was supposed to come, show the world she supported him, and meet his family. It would be a huge step for her, for them. He was almost as nervous for her as he was to play this game, but he knew his family would love her. How could anyone resist his beautiful Cambree?

Riker Dylan, the quarterback, slapped him on the shoulder, taking his attention from his family and that vacant seat. "You ready to catch bullets all day?"

"I hate to flex on ya, but I can catch any wild pass you want to loft my way."

Riker laughed. "Don't worry. My perfect spiral could be caught by a five-year-old."

Emmett smiled back. "Good, send those one's X's way. X has been married too long and he's getting soft. He's only still on the team because he married the owner's daughter."

Xavier Newton came up behind him and thumped him on the head. It echoed in his helmet. "I heard that. You're lucky I don't blow out your other knee."

"I saw you there," Emmett said.

"Yeah, right. Besides, it's Brady who gets all the favors with Papa Knight," X insisted.

"Ha! I heard the press release—old James Knight bragging about how you're the best husband and daddy he's ever seen."

"That's 'cause I got the prettiest wife and baby girl in the world." X puffed out his chest and grinned. "You wanna see pictures?"

"Guys. Head in the game," one of the coaches said from behind them.

They all laughed and tightened their helmet straps.

The Storm's kicker lofted the ball in the air, and the Titans' kick receiver got a respectable thirty yards off the return. The hometown crowd roared in approval.

Emmett cast one more glance over his shoulder as the receiving team ran off and he prepared to run on with the offense. Right between his mom and Bridger, the sun seemed to shine on the spot where Cambree's dark curls sprung around her beautiful face and cascaded down her back. She saw him and jabbed both fists in the air. He couldn't hear her over the booming crowd, but he could see her mouth moving and thought she was saying, "My bossy man!"

He grinned and ran for his position. This was going to be his best game ever.

Cambree's palms were sweating as a man in a suit escorted her down the stands toward Emmett's family's seats. She loved that they sat in the front row and not in some stuffy box, putting themselves above the crowd, but she was so nervous to meet them. What if they already hated her? Her mama had been given plenty of awkward media opportunities over the past two months, and Cambree had also responded too honestly a time or two that her relationship with Emmett was none of the reporter's "busybody busy-ness." The media had a heyday with that one.

She pressed down her floral sundress, feeling pretty and poised with her hair in smooth curls down her back. She'd tried her best to look the part of an NFL player's girlfriend, but she'd bought her dress at Target and didn't have any plastic parts or two-hundred-dollar haircut. What if they all saw right through her attempts to fit in? What if she offended his family somehow? She wanted them to like her.

The pressure of being Emmett's girlfriend was hard sometimes, but he was worth it and he never put pressure on her to change. They'd only seen each other in person a few times since her Warrior race when he'd come for her and declared his love, but they texted and talked every day and she loved him. She had also learned to trust him. He didn't care what anyone thought—well, except for her. He was definitely not Nolan, and he'd proved he wouldn't dump her for saying something wrong. If only she could earn his family's approval. If by some miracle they'd like her for her.

"This is your seat, ma'am." The escort smiled to her and gestured past him. Five sets of deep brown eyes swung to stare at her. She felt awful that she was late. She'd stood at the top of the stadium with her hand over her heart for the national anthem. Tears had streamed down her face as the big screen showed Emmett and his teammates standing so respectfully and the announcer talked about Creed Hawk and his SEAL Team, who had given their lives for America.

She raised a hand. "Hi," she said, walking unsteadily toward Emmett's family. "It's terrifying to finally meet you." At least she knew them all from pictures and Emmett's stories.

Bridger threw back his head and laughed. He wrapped an arm around her and gave her a squeeze. "Just stay close to me. I'm the nonthreatening one."

"Thanks." She brushed her hand across her forehead. "Whew."

Callum extended his hand. "Pleasure to meet you, Ms. Kinley."

Cambree shook his hand, all stiff and awkward.

"He's the one you have to be afraid of," Bridger said out of the side of his mouth.

"You stop it," said Emmett's mom, Caroline. She grabbed Cambree in a tight hug. "My girl," she gushed. "Are you going to marry my boy so I'm finally not the only woman in this crazy crew?"

Cambree's mouth dropped open. "And I thought I was too blunt," she couldn't help but say.

"No, our Mom will embarrass you as much as possible," Bridger explained.

Caroline swatted him on the shoulder. "You watch it or I'll ... I won't make you snickerdoodles next time you come see me."

Bridger's eyes widened. "All right. I'll be good." He shuddered. "She can make some vicious threats, so watch yourself."

Emmett's dad extended his hand. "Thomas Hawk."

Cambree shook his hand. "Tomahawk?" she asked.

Bridger laughed so loud, it drowned out the crowd's cheering about the kickoff return. "We used to call him that behind his back."

Thomas shot Bridger a look, but he smiled at Cambree. "I'd prefer Tom."

"Okay, I can do that."

"Hey, your man's looking for you," Bridger said.

Cambree's eyes pivoted to the field and locked onto Emmett. Whoa. He looked even bigger and tougher than normal with all his pads and helmet on. She jabbed her fists in the air and yelled, "My bossy man!"

He grinned, waved, and then ran onto the field. His family all got settled and she found herself sitting between Caroline and Bridger, which made her a lot more comfortable. Especially as the game progressed and Caroline, in her fancy pink short-sleeved jacket, skirt, and heels, kept leaping to her feet and yelling like a drunken sailor. She was hilarious and so into the game. Cambree loved it.

She especially loved watching Emmett. He'd worked so hard to get his knee up to full strength, and he'd really made a comeback. He and Riker Dylan were in sync, Riker would throw the ball quick and hard and Emmett would run the perfect pattern to snatch the ball and sprint until he got tackled. She hated watching the other team slam him into the turf, but he was tough and always sprung back up, and often it looked like he was bantering with the guy who tackled him.

At halftime, someone brought a bunch of food and drinks to the family, right there on the front row. Cambree noticed a lot of pictures being snapped by other fans of her and Emmett's family. She didn't like it, but she'd deal with it ... for Emmett. He'd taught her more about trust and bravery in the past month than anyone had in her whole life. She was strong enough to handle a little media pressure, especially if it meant she could be with Emmett. After the game, she would be able to spend tonight and tomorrow with Emmett before she flew back to teach on Tuesday. Thank heavens it was Labor Day weekend.

She talked easily with Bridger, Caroline, and even Tom. Callum was a little standoffish, but she mostly ignored him. He spent a lot of the game on his phone, either taking calls or tapping away at something more important than his family.

Some of the men behind them were obviously drinking too much. One of them knocked his beer over at halftime and it hit the back of Cambree's calves as she was standing to stretch.

When she whirled around in surprise, he leered at her. "Hey, I've seen you on TV. You're the gold digger that's after Emmett Hawk."

Cambree sucked in a breath and put her hand on her stomach. Should she lay this guy out, or walk away? How should Emmett Hawk's girlfriend respond?

The guy's eyes roved over her. "You are hot, but Emmett could do much better than trailer trash."

She thought maybe the guy deserved a punch to the gut like she'd given Nolan. Smiling, she knew Emmett would approve of anything she did.

"Excuse me." Callum was at her elbow. "What's your name, sir?"

The guy blinked at him. "Joe Klein."

Callum tapped something into his phone. "Joe Klein. Got it. Expect to hear from our lawyers about a defamation suit."

"What?" The guy exploded and stood, leaning across the chair back. "Don't you threaten me."

Bridger was at her other side now. Both Bridger and Callum were almost as nicely built as Emmett and looked like twin bodyguards, sandwiching her between them and protecting her like only Emmett would do.

The guy scuttled back a step, running into his own seat.

"Nobody slanders our brother's girlfriend," Callum said calmly. He arched an eyebrow. "Are we clear?"

The guy nodded and slumped into his seat.

Bridger turned Cambree back around with his arm around her shoulder. "You okay?" he asked. "Your body's doing the mamba."

She hadn't realized she was shaking. "Yeah." She glanced up at Callum. "Thank you."

"Not a problem." Callum smiled at her. "We're happy you're here." Then he went back to tapping on his phone.

Callum had stood up for her. It was unexpected and appreciated. Maybe other people, like the jerk behind her, thought she wasn't worthy of Emmett, but his family didn't act like that. Quite the opposite—they accepted her wholeheartedly. Warmth rushed through her. Maybe she *could* be part of the Hawk family. The guy behind them had been a jerk, but Callum and Bridger had acted like she was their sister and stood up for her.

Bridger gave her shoulder a squeeze and kept his arm around her until the game started again and she didn't feel like everyone around them was staring at her. Luckily Emmett's parents had been distracted talking to the people sitting on their other side, so she didn't think they'd noticed the ugly interaction. She felt like the guy's eyes were boring into her from behind, but she ignored him and focused on the game.

The game was great, besides that one idiot. The Titans won 21-7. The crowd roared their approval and Emmett's mom hollered and yelled. After he shook the other team's hands, Emmett took off his helmet and sprinted their direction.

"That's my boy!" Caroline yelled.

Emmett was grinning as he ran at them, dropped his helmet, hit the wall eight feet below them, and launched himself up. He grasped the handrail and pulled himself up in front of them.

The fans behind them were screaming his name and his family was cheering and laughing, but Emmett was focused completely on Cambree. "You made it," he said.

"You think I'd miss this party?" she asked.

"There's a ticket with your name on it for every game."

"Hmm. We'll see if I can fit you in my schedule."

"You'd better fit me in. I'm your boyfriend and I want the whole world to know it."

Cambree laughed. "I thought I had to agree to be your girlfriend."

"Give it to him, sista!" Bridger called out.

"Shush," Caroline said. "I want to watch this."

Cambree blushed. She'd forgotten they had a crowd.

Emmett cocked his head. "Let me see if I can convince you." He vaulted himself over the bars and wrapped her up in his arms. He was bulky with all the pads and he was dripping with sweat, but Cambree didn't care. He'd held her for hours sweaty and muddy after her Warrior race. Emmett really did want to claim her before the world and she found she wanted the same thing. Nolan's rejection couldn't affect her any more. She was stronger than that and was grateful that because of that pain, she now had something beautiful: Emmett.

He bent down close and she arched up on tiptoes. His lips met hers and he set to work convincing her. Cambree could hear the bellow of the crowd around them and she finally pulled back, staring into his dark eyes. "I love you, Emmett Hawk."

"I love you too, Cambree Kinley."

"Hey, you two are on the jumbotron," Bridger said.

Cambree tried to pull back, but Emmett didn't release her. "So do you approve of my crazy family?" he asked like they weren't being videoed for the entire stadium to gawk at.

Cambree laughed. "I think I take the cake on the crazy family. Your family is perfect."

"You'd better claim her, bro," Bridger put in. "She told me I'm the backup plan."

Emmett growled. "You'd better stay back or I'll thump you good."

"I'd like to see you try."

"Boys," Caroline cautioned. She put a hand on Emmett's arm. "She's a doll, Emmett. Great game, my boy. I'm so proud."

Emmett released Cambree from the hug to enfold his mom in his arms. "Thanks for being here."

"You know I'd never miss a game." She pushed at him. "You stink, my love."

"Cam didn't seem to mind." He winked at her. He shook his dad's and Callum's hands, receiving their congrats, then put Bridger in a headlock.

Cambree glanced around and noticed they had a pretty good crowd around them. Luckily the guy who made fun of her earlier was nowhere to be seen. Little kids held out footballs and papers to be autographed as their parents watched with smiles.

Emmett glanced at her. "I'm gonna work this crowd, then go shower. I'll see you later?"

"If I'm impressed by your crowd-working."

He grinned and gave her one more quick kiss, then slipped around her to start signing autographs. He was so comfortable and confident. Her stomach swooped, and she worried again if she could really do this, really be the girlfriend of a superstar like Emmett. Then he glanced back at her with a huge grin, and she had to return that smile. It was a special smile, reserved for the woman he loved—her.

Caroline put her arm around Cambree's waist. "Will you come with us to dinner? We're going to Los Tios. It's kind of a staple with the Titans. Emmett will meet us there."

"I'd love to." She glanced at Emmett again. "I bet you're bursting with pride," she said to his mom.

Caroline beamed at her. "Yes, I am." She lowered her voice.

"And I'm praying you'll say yes when he proposes. I know how much he loves you, and I already love you too."

Cambree had to blink at the sudden tears forming in her eyes. She'd been worried if this classy lady would even accept her, but Emmett's mother was so filled with love she was impossible to resist. "Thank you, Caroline."

"Thank you, darling girl. We've needed the happiness you've brought us today ... after losing Creed."

She couldn't imagine the hole in this woman's heart, losing her son, but she was gracious, warm, and welcoming. Cambree couldn't resist giving her another hug. They were both teary-eyed when they pulled away. Caroline squeezed her hand and gave her a trembling smile then turned to her husband.

Tom put his arm around Caroline and escorted her up the steps. Callum gestured for Cambree to go ahead. He was on his phone again, but he did offer Cambree a welcoming smile, and she'd never forget how he defended her earlier. Bridger offered his arm and Cambree walked up the steps with Emmett's family. She, Cambree Kinley, felt like a part of the renowned Hawk family. All because of Emmett. She hated being separated for him for a moment, but as she glanced back and saw him ruffling a small boy's hair as the boy beamed up at him, she knew he needed to be where he was. She'd get time with him tonight, away from the cameras. If the happy bubbles in her stomach were any indication, tonight was going to be fabulous.

CHAPTER SEVENTEEN

Cambree slipped her high-heeled sandals off and sank into Emmett's leather sofa. The view from his downtown Dallas condo was unreal, high above the entire city, the lights sparkling far below.

"So this is how the richie half live, eh?" she asked.

Emmett sat next to her and handed her a water bottle.

"Thanks," she said, taking a long drink. The dinner with his family had been fun, lots of teasing and stories, and even when she said something too blunt, they all laughed and seemed to like her. Even Callum relaxed a little bit and put his phone away during dinner. Callum's show of support at the game had really endeared him to her, and proven to her that she could allow herself to trust Emmett's family to treat her like an equal and be there for her.

"You like it?" Emmett gestured to the view.

Cambree turned and focused on his handsome face. "Very much."

Emmett grinned and leaned closer, softly kissing her.

"I like that very much too," she muttered against his lips. "Especially since you don't smell like my brother's hockey gear he hasn't washed in two years anymore."

"Oh, ouch." Emmett put a hand to his chest. "I was that bad after the game?"

Cambree laughed. "You were close, but I can take a little stink."

Emmett set his water bottle on the coffee table and took hers also and set it down. He wrapped his arm around her waist and pulled her closer. "You're the toughest woman I know. I think you could handle anything."

Cambree bit at her lip. "You think pretty highly of me, but I don't know if I can handle all of this." She gestured around at the condo that was nicer than any place she'd ever seen, including his high-dollar fitness camp.

Emmett studied her. "Cam. If you want me to sell all my houses and live in a trailer like your mama, I would do it for you."

"H-houses?" she squeaked out.

He nodded.

"Where are these ..." She gulped. "Houses?"

Emmett pressed his lips together, then finally spilled out, "Sun Valley, Park City, Maui, and Costa Rica."

"Hmm. So lots of snow-skiing and lots of beach time?"

He nodded.

"And you'd give all that up ... for me?"

"In a second."

Cambree stared at him, her heart thumping quicker and quicker. "Ah, you sweetie." She cupped his cheek and kissed him once softly, then harder. Emmett pulled her in tight and kissed her and kissed her and kissed her. His mouth was demanding yet gentle. When he deepened the kiss, her stomach smoldered with heat.

Cambree finally came up for air and had to rearrange her hair back out of her face. "Whew, you do know how to heat a body up."

Emmett threw back his head and laughed. "And you do know how to make me so happy." He lifted her onto his lap and trailed kisses along her neck before capturing her mouth again. Cambree clung to his strong shoulders and enjoyed every movement of his lips and his hands.

"Marry me?" he murmured against her lips.

Cambree drew back quickly, gasping. "Wh-what? We haven't dated long enough to—"

Emmett cut her protests off with another kiss, even more intense than the last. He deepened the kiss and the pleasure receptors in her mouth went nuts. She had no clue which way was up when he released her mouth and whispered, "Please marry me, sweetheart."

Cambree tickled her fingers through his hair and stared at his handsome face. "If you'll promise to tattoo 'Cambree's bossy man' across your forehead."

Emmett whooped and laughed. "Done!"

"I was joking. I don't want any tattoos on this perfect face. Maybe across your chest, but ... hmm, wait, that's perfect also." She winked and cupped his cheeks with her hands, loving the short hair under her palms.

"I hate needles, but I'd do anything for you, Cam."

"Wimp." She smiled as she ran her fingers down across his shoulders. He was the toughest man she'd ever met. "I'm super proud of you, by the way. You showed everyone how tough you were today."

"Thanks. It was a hard game, but it felt great too." He got a mischievous grin. "I'm always 'super proud' of you, but I'd be prouder of you if you'd agree to marry me."

"Then I guess I'd better make you the proudest man in the world and say yes."

"Yes?"

Cambree took a breath and closed her eyes. She opened them to study his handsome face. His dark eyes so full of yearning ... for her. "Yes," she whispered.

"Yes!" He punched a fist in the air. "That's my girl." He tucked her in close for a kiss she would always treasure.

His words rang through her head. She was his, and he was definitely hers. The only things sweeter than those truths were the tantalizing kisses he bestowed on her.

Hawk Brothers Romance

The Determined Groom

The Stealth Warrior

Her Billionaire Boss Fake Fiance

Risking it All

EXCERPT: THE STEALTH WARRIOR

After finishing her exhausting performance, all Kiera wanted to do was take a shower and order room service. She exited the stage area and headed toward her building. A hand on her arm stopped her. Whirling around, she came face to face with the blond man she'd danced with tonight.

"Hello, beautiful." He had an English accent and a smooth tongue.

Kiera gave him a forced smile. "Excuse me," she murmured. She'd told enough yahoos "not interested" to understand you had to keep it short and sweet and move away quick.

"Wait." He tightened his hold on her arm. It wasn't painful, but it was clear he wanted to be in charge. "Fancy a bit of late supper?"

Kiera shook her head. "Sorry." He looked too old for her, probably late thirties or early forties, definitely some plastic surgery. The man was handsome, and she liked his accent, but she wasn't partial to blond men. Dark hair, dark eyes, and tanned skin with short facial hair. There she went picturing Creed, as usual. He'd made it more than obvious he didn't want her when he'd returned from the dead. Months had passed, and the cretin still hadn't so much as called her. She knew Creed could track a shark through the ocean. If he wanted to, he would've found her on her travels through Thailand, the Philippines, Africa, and now the Caribbean.

The beautiful, innocent children on her service trips had helped her push her pain to the back of her mind. Yet her heart would never heal. If only she could tell her heart to forget about Creed. Sadly, hearts didn't work like that.

"Maybe tomorrow?" The man persisted.

"Maybe." She nodded to him and walked past. She didn't think he followed, but as she walked along the dimly-lit pathways back to her suite, she could sense someone was following her. She thought about calling security, but for some reason, she wasn't afraid. She could simply sense a presence.

Maybe someone from the show was enamored with her. She'd been a big name once. Now, she was a washed-up has been. Lately, she'd focused on charity performances, and though she hadn't been able to forget Creed, she'd thoroughly enjoyed seeing new lands and meeting the people, especially the children. She'd also worked at several gorgeous resorts like this. The pay was fine at the resorts, nothing close to what she'd made when she'd starred in Vegas, L.A., London, and New York, but she didn't really care much about the pay. She was happy to be far from America and the painful memories of Creed.

She took the elevator to her twelfth-floor penthouse suite. The resort treated her like she was still something special and had told her she could stay as long as she wanted. She only had to do the performance every few nights. They had a lot of other entertainment coming in.

Finally entering her room, she slid out of her heels, slipped her dress over her head and took a long shower before sliding into a floral, silk robe and blow drying her hair quickly and tying it back in a ponytail. She grabbed the room service menu. Supposedly, the Japanese restaurant was to die for. She could really go for a dragon roll and a crazy boy with no siracha right now. Ooh, and a shrimp tempura appetizer. She dialed room service and placed an order for way too much food, knowing she would never eat it all. She'd lost too much weight when Creed died and still struggled to eat a full meal.

Kiera stretched out on the king-sized bed in the master bedroom and sighed. It was comfy. Maybe she would take a short nap before dinner. Then she would stay up reading or watching a movie or something. What did she have to do tomorrow besides exercise and lay on the beach, being gracious to tourists who recognized her? She used to practice twelve to fourteen hours a day, but maintaining her fitness level was enough for the type of dancing she was doing currently.

There was a sharp rap at the door. That was quick. Kiera pushed off the bed and tightened the robe. She hurried to the door and opened it a crack. Glancing out, she expected to see dinner containers and a smiling attendant. Instead, she saw a glowering man with dark hair, dark eyes, tanned skin, and the perfect length of facial hair.

"Creed?" The world started spinning around her, and then everything went black.

She crumpled to the floor but could hear a voice floating

above her. A voice she'd dreamed of hearing so often she knew it couldn't be reality. The voice came from far above, just like Creed was far away and would never be here for her again.

"Kiera? Kiera?" Creed's voice finally registered. It had to be him. She knew that voice like she knew her dance routines.

Kiera shook her head. She'd really lost it now. She'd dreamed Creed was at her door, and now, she was hearing his voice.

The door pushed softly against her, and she stirred, scrambling away from it.

"Kiera?" Creed truly stood above her in the doorway.

No. Creed coming for her was a dream she'd burned months ago, okay maybe weeks, but she had finally burned it and locked her heart away from the pain. Hadn't she?

He pushed the door open a little farther and slipped inside. The door closed behind him, and Kiera couldn't budge from off the floor. She stared up at his perfect face. She'd forgotten how huge he was—almost six four. He had so much muscle it made her mouth go dry. The white shirt showed off his tanned skin, and a few undone buttons revealed his muscular chest.

She shook her head. She must be in shock. Creed couldn't be here. Creed had ditched her and didn't love her. Why would he follow her to Cancun? He had much more important jobs to do other than tracking her down.

Creed bent down, wrapped his hands around her waist and easily plucked her to her feet. She'd been lifted so many times in her career, sometimes even pretending to be vulnerable or wounded for her part, but she'd assisted her partner with every lift. Creed had just lifted her as a dead weight. He was impossibly strong, and she was like a limp noodle. She leaned heavily against him.

"Kiera." His voice went all soft and husky, and the way he was studying her made her feel warm and prickly from head to toe. Oh, how she'd loved him.

He wrapped his arms around her back and gently pulled her close. Kiera had no clue how to respond to this very real-feeling hallucination. "C-creed," she whispered, not returning his hug, but loving the feel of his muscled chest pressing against her.

"Now come on, love. You can do better than that."

"What?" She was so confused. She stared up into his dark eyes, and they were twinkling at her like they always used to do. All the angst, pain, and confusion of losing him disappeared and there was just her and Creed. No matter what had come between them before they were together now. It was so simple and beautiful.

"This is *not* a hug. A hug involves two bodies, four arms, and lots and lots of contact." He winked. "Shall we give it another go?"

Tears sprang from her eyes as she stared at his handsome face and charming smile. She threw her arms around his neck and clung to him. Creed had said a similar line to her the very first time he hugged her. She'd been young and had never even held hands with a boy. She'd felt extremely awkward when the cutest boy at school had given her attention then hugged her at a party after a home football game.

"Ah, that's better." Creed groaned, and the warmth and desire in that groan filled her stomach with heat.

Kiera thought it was more than better. It was absolute perfection. Her head fit in the crook of his neck like they were built to come together. *Creed!* Her heart seemed to be cheering. Creed was truly here and holding her like she'd dreamed of so many times. It had taken him too long to find her, but he'd finally come for her and that was all that mattered.

He ran his hands along her back, and it felt like heaven with the silk sliding against her skin and Creed's warm hands doing a number on her nervous system. He brought one hand up and loosened her ponytail then trailed his fingers through her hair. "Kiera."

Kiera stared up at him as he bowed his head closer to hers. His mint-tinged breath and his warm, sensuous cologne made her stomach flutter. It was the cologne she'd bought him for Christmas one year—Burberry. It had a great mix of cinnamon, amber, and tarragon and made her want to melt every time she smelled it on him.

Creed was here. He was alive, and he was holding her. His breath brushed her lips, and Kiera sighed with longing. How she'd missed him, missed his touch. She arched up to kiss him as he whispered, "Oh man, I'm going to regret this in the morning."

Then he was kissing her, and her brain couldn't process anything but the pressure of his lips on hers. They'd been made to kiss each other. There was nothing on Earth she loved more than dancing except this. Creed always had a rhythm to his kisses, a natural and instinctive choreography, and tonight was the perfect arrangement for her. He started hard and fast, capturing her lips and conveying how he'd hungered for her. How they'd been apart for far too long. She returned the hunger and then some. This kiss was the kiss of a warrior who had won the battle and was back to claim what was due to him. Kiera should've protested that she wasn't the girl waiting for the hunky hero anymore, but there was no strength in her to protest, only to savor and fully return his mind-blowing kiss.

After several blissful, heat-filled minutes, he slowed the kisses down and took his time exploring her lips and mouth. It was like he was tasting her and savoring her and couldn't get enough. Kiera's body hummed with awareness and desire from her mouth out. She could never get enough of him. Finally, the pain of separation, the waiting to be together was over. She was right where she was meant to be—in Creed's arms and being swept away by his kisses.

Kiera's head was so cloudy and full of Creed that she couldn't stand on her own two feet. Luckily, she didn't need to with his strong arms holding her close, burning fire through her thin robe. She held on tight to his broad back and let him work his magic on her mouth.

His lips left hers and slowly trailed down her neck, leaving fire in their wake. He was working his way back up to her lips, and she could hardly stand the wait, but then he broke away and straightened, muttering, "I can't do this."

Kiera blinked at him, confused and wanting him to keep kissing her. He couldn't do ... what exactly? He stepped back, released his hold on her and shoved a hand through his hair, staring broodily down at her.

He said nothing, and Kiera was chilled and shaky, swaying on her feet. She'd been ripped too quickly from his heat and touch. It was like being in a steam room then jumping into an ice-cold pool. Her head cleared bit by bit, and she thought of what he'd said right before he kissed her. "Why are you going to regret kissing me in the morning?"

Creed blew out a breath, and now instead of broody, he was openly glaring at her. "You need to put some clothes on."

Kiera reared back and glanced down at her robe. It covered her, going clear down to her knees with double sashes at her waist that were both tied tight. Most of her stage costumes were more revealing. She folded her arms across her chest and glared at him. "No. Right now, you need to explain ... lots of things."

Creed glanced at her robe before meeting her gaze. "*I* need to explain?" He put a hand to his chest. "That's exactly what I was thinking. *I'm* the one who needs to explain."

The sarcasm dripped from his voice, but she wasn't about to back down. "Exactly," she said, not giving an inch. "You can start with why you 'can't do this,' said right after we kissed. Then explain 'I'm going to regret this in the morning' being said right before we kissed. Then we can go back to hmm, I don't know, you being not dead and never coming for me, and making me wish you *were* dead!" She pushed out a frustrated breath, clenching her fists when she wanted to pound on his chest. Yet she didn't trust herself to touch him right now. Too much risk of getting lost in him again and losing her well-deserved anger.

"Why are you even here?" she shot at him.

Creed gave her a dry chuckle. "I'm not here to talk to you Kiera, and I'm definitely not here to kiss you. I'm here to give you a warning."

Kiera's heart had already shriveled and died when he was confirmed dead, but when he came back to life and never came for her, her heart turned into a rock. Somehow, miraculously it could still hurt though. This wasn't him coming for her. Of course, it wasn't. He regretted even kissing her. Why was she even surprised?

"I'm a big girl. I can take care of myself without Mr. Bad-A Navy SEAL taking pity on my sorry self and coming to watch out for me."

Creed took a step closer to her. Kiera stood her ground. The man who used to love and adore her was now trying to intimidate her. Why had she loved this cretin so desperately? She glanced over his beautifully-sculpted face and body. Besides his irresistible looks, he used to be fun, smart, charming, and nice. Now, he was simply the man who had never cared about her enough to return to her. The man who had killed her heart.

"Stay away from the older blond guy. The one with the lame English accent."

It was easy to know who he meant. There'd only been a few blond men at the show tonight, only one she'd danced with, and only one who had an accent.

"Didn't seem much older to me, pretty hot and fit actually."

Creed's jaw clamped tight, and a muscle worked in it. Kiera wanted to reach up and touch his jaw. Tell him she'd do what he asked if only he'd hold her again. She clamped her arms tighter around herself.

"Don't you dare, Kiera. You just try and date him, and you'll see what kind of a bad-A Navy SEAL I am."

If she wasn't so ticked at him, he would be inspiring to behold right now. All that muscle and raw determination. She could feel the strength radiating from him. She'd never been afraid of Creed, never would be, but she could imagine if someone was on his wrong side they'd be in peril.

Yet he had no desire to be with her, and the blond guy seemed to tick him off. Hmm. She wasn't above using that to tick him off more. Turnabout was fair play. She'd been broken since he rejected her without having the guts to actually do it face to face. Simply sending her some Dear Jane letter that she'd wrongly assumed meant he loved her and wanted her happiness above all else. Now, she realized it was just a cop-out. *Go live your life, go be happy*. Then the dream-ruiner had been brought back to life and run away on his "missions." He'd left her with nothing, her and her stone of a heart.

A rap came at the door, and Creed glowered at her. "Expecting someone?"

"Actually, I was." She raised an eyebrow and watched the emotions race across his face—anger and jealousy warring with one another. Maybe there was something left in him that cared about her.

She pushed around him to get the door. Creed caught her arm and pulled her back against his chest. The breath rushed out of her. She molded to his body perfectly. His arms came around her waist, and Kiera couldn't help but sigh with longing for him. The thin robe wasn't nearly enough to protect her from the heat and possessiveness of his arms. The exquisite strength of his chest muscles pressing against her back.

He bent close and whispered in her ear, "Who's at the door, Kiera?"

Kiera tilted her head to meet his dark gaze and gave him a look full of challenge. Let him think she'd invited a room full of men over for all she cared. "Something I've been craving all day," she whispered.

His eyes darkened to almost black, and his arms tightened around her. If she wasn't so ticked off, she would've loved every second of being this close to Creed. The protectiveness and desire in his embrace were so familiar yet thrilling. She'd been without him, craved him, for too long, and she was in danger of falling for him all over again.

"You'd better ask him to leave unless you want to watch me decimate the man on your doorstep," he threatened in a low growl.

"I don't think you even understand who you're competing with." She gave him a condescending glare.

"No one stands a chance against me."

Kiera thought that was probably true. The knock came again.

"Who is it Kiera?" Creed's eyes were narrowed and full of protective intent. Kiera wanted to tell him that he had no right to be protective of her anymore, but she worried about pushing him too far, afraid for the poor room service attendant on the other side of the door.

She looked into Creed's gaze and whispered back, "Room service."

Creed stared in disbelief. Then he started laughing. She loved the rumble of laughter in his chest pressing against her back. Kiera couldn't help but laugh along with him.

"I thought ..." He shook his head and released her.

Kiera's laughter died quickly. She wasn't sure she wanted to know what he'd thought, and she hated that him touching her again was a craving she would never be able to satiate.

She went and opened the door. A smiling young man rolled the serving dolly in and unloaded several trays onto the table.

"Gracias," Kiera said.

Creed palmed him a twenty, and the young man walked out the door grinning.

"You're not supposed to tip them. They were very specific about that when I checked in."

"None of them have complained yet," Creed said.

"You don't need to act like a billionaire."

He didn't even respond. He stared over the various plates of food with a furrowed brow. The anger was back in his eyes, and she wasn't sure why. Hadn't they just laughed together? It didn't change anything, couldn't fix the pain of him not wanting her, but couldn't they somehow, someway talk this out? No. Nothing he could say would make up for the way he'd deserted her. Him dying had been horrific, but she'd never blamed him. Him being brought back to life but not coming for her? That she blamed him for aplenty. Yet what if he'd been tortured so horribly it had ruined his mind and his ability to love? Maybe that was why he didn't want her anymore. Being around him right now, he seemed like the old Creed. Her Creed. No. She couldn't think like that ever again.

Creed uncovered platters, and a ghost of a smile touched his lips. "You and your sushi." Then the smile was gone. "Who are you expecting, Kiera?"

She stared at him. "What?"

Creed strode away from the table and got right in her space. Kiera did back away this time. Creed kept coming until she was backed into a wall.

"The Kiera I knew would never order this much food, knowing she could only eat a fraction of it. The Kiera I knew hated to waste. She was too worried about those who didn't have enough food. Taught well by her philanthropist mama."

He didn't know her anymore, and even though her breath was coming in fast pants from his nearness, he was ticking her off. She wished her body didn't respond to him so readily, like muscle memory. It reminded her of dancing the merengue, so easy a drunk person could do it and so natural as soon as the music started playing you couldn't help but dance along. Creed came near, and her body immediately flooded with heat and wanted to touch him and move in rhythm with him.

"You don't know me anymore," she whispered, getting caught up in his dark, stormy gaze.

Creed swallowed, and his body brushed against hers. "That's for sure." He stepped back and glowered at her. "I'm only going to ask one more time. Who were you expecting ... wearing that?" His eyes traveled over her robe.

"I'm only going to ask once. Get out." She pointed at the door. Unfortunately, her hand was shaking. Why was Creed acting like she was some loose woman? They'd made a pact in high school to never let the fire of their love get out of control, to save themselves for marriage. He'd tried a few times to push farther than they should, and she'd helped him stay in control. The night before he left, it was her that had tried to get him to break the pact, and he'd stayed strong. Their love was stronger than a mere physical bond. That's what he always said when they were tempted. Creed had to know she wouldn't be waiting for someone in her suite in nothing but a robe.

Creed blinked at her and bent down close again. "I thought what we used to have was special to you, but obviously, you aren't the Kiera I fell in love with."

Kiera slapped him across the face. The slap rang through the room, and neither of them moved. Creed finally gave her his sarcastic smile. The one he gave to people he hated. "This isn't over, Kiera. I'll be watching you, and I'll protect you. Even if you don't care about protecting yourself any longer."

Kiera's stomach felt sick, and she knew all this food was going to go to waste. Her mama would be disappointed in her right now for more reasons than that. "Do I need to slap you again? Or are you leaving?"

Creed stormed to the door and threw it open. He turned and threw verbal daggers back at her. "I despise what you've become, Kiera, but if you ever cared for me at all, stay away from the blond guy."

Kiera hurried to the door and pushed at him. He didn't budge an inch. "Get out!" she screamed.

Creed smiled at her. "I'll get out, but if any other man tries to come through this door, I'll tear him apart. Sleep tight." He waved and stepped out onto the wide patio.

Kiera slammed the door shut and screamed a gargled, "Argh! I hate you Creed Hawk!"

She could hear his laughter on the other side of the door. Running to the bedroom, she threw herself down on the bed. Anger still rushed through her, but the sadness wasn't far behind. Creed was here. He hadn't come for her. He didn't care about her. And now, for some reason, he thought she was a floozy. There had been those rumors of her and Milo living together, but Creed wouldn't believe that kind of smut. At least, her Creed wouldn't. He'd really said that he despised what she'd become. What kind of rotten thing was that to say? Why had he kissed her like that? Just to torture her and make her see all she was missing not being in his arms? Tears wet the pillow beneath her face. She had loved him for so long and so deeply, he'd been her inspiration and her every dream. Now everything they'd once shared was tainted and ugly.

She brushed the tears off and made a promise to herself. Next time the blond English guy asked her to dinner, she was going. She could only pray Creed would go insane with jealousy. He obviously didn't love her anymore, and she had no clue why he was treating her so horribly, but she could see the jealousy on his face, and he'd kissed her like he still wanted her. Even if all she had was the ability to make him hurt like he'd hurt her. She would take it.

Hawk Brothers Romance

The Determined Groom

The Stealth Warrior

Her Billionaire Boss Fake Fiance

Risking it All

ALSO BY CAMI CHECKETTS

The Hidden Kingdom Romances

Royal Secrets

Royal Security

Royal Doctor

Royal Mistake

Royal Courage

Royal Pilot

Royal Imposter

Royal Baby

Royal Battle

Royal Fake Fiancé

Secret Valley Romance

Sister Pact

Marriage Pact

Christmas Pact

Famous Friends Romances

Loving the Firefighter

Loving the Athlete

Loving the Rancher

Loving the Coach

Loving the Sheriff

Loving the Contractor

Loving the Entertainer

Running Romcom

Running for Love

Taken from Love

Saved by Love

Survive the Romance

Romancing the Treasure

Romancing the Escape

Romancing the Boat

Romancing the Mountain

Romancing the Castle

Romancing the Extreme Adventure

Romancing the Island

Romancing the River

Romancing the Spartan Race

Mystical Lake Resort Romance

Only Her Undercover Spy

Only Her Cowboy

Only Her Best Friend

Only Her Blue-Collar Billionaire

Only Her Injured Stuntman

Only Her Amnesiac Fake Fiancé

Only Her Hockey Legend

Only Her Smokejumper Firefighter

Only Her Christmas Miracle

Jewel Family Romance

Do Marry Your Billionaire Boss

Do Trust Your Special Ops Bodyguard

Do Date Your Handsome Rival

Do Rely on Your Protector

Do Kiss the Superstar

Do Tease the Charming Billionaire

Do Claim the Tempting Athlete

Do Depend on Your Keeper

Strong Family Romance

Don't Date Your Brother's Best Friend

Her Loyal Protector

Don't Fall for a Fugitive

Her Hockey Superstar Fake Fiance

Don't Ditch a Detective

Don't Miss the Moment

Don't Love an Army Ranger

Don't Chase a Player

Don't Abandon the Superstar

Steele Family Romance

Her Dream Date Boss

The Stranded Patriot

The Committed Warrior

Extreme Devotion

Quinn Family Romance

The Devoted Groom

The Conflicted Warrior

The Gentle Patriot

The Tough Warrior

Her Too-Perfect Boss

Her Forbidden Bodyguard

Cami's Collections

Survive the Romance Collection

Mystical Lake Resort Romance Collection

Billionaire Boss Romance Collection

Jewel Family Collection

The Romance Escape Collection

Cami's Firefighter Collection

Strong Family Romance Collection

Steele Family Collection

Hawk Brothers Collection

Quinn Family Collection

Cami's Georgia Patriots Collection

Cami's Military Collection

Billionaire Beach Romance Collection

Billionaire Bride Pact Collection

Echo Ridge Romance Collection

Texas Titans Romance Collection

Snow Valley Collection

Christmas Romance Collection

Holiday Romance Collection

Extreme Sports Romance Collection

Georgia Patriots Romance

The Loyal Patriot

The Gentle Patriot

The Stranded Patriot

The Pursued Patriot

Jepson Brothers Romance

How to Design Love

How to Switch a Groom

How to Lose a Fiance

Billionaire Boss Romance

Her Dream Date Boss

Her Prince Charming Boss

Hawk Brothers Romance

The Determined Groom

The Stealth Warrior

Her Billionaire Boss Fake Fiance

Risking it All

Navy Seal Romance

The Protective Warrior

The Captivating Warrior

The Stealth Warrior

The Tough Warrior

Texas Titan Romance

The Fearless Groom

The Trustworthy Groom

The Beastly Groom

The Irresistible Groom

The Determined Groom

The Devoted Groom

Billionaire Beach Romance

Caribbean Rescue

Cozumel Escape

Cancun Getaway

Trusting the Billionaire

How to Kiss a Billionaire

Onboard for Love

Shadows in the Curtain

Billionaire Bride Pact Romance

The Resilient One

The Feisty One

The Independent One

The Protective One

The Faithful One

The Daring One

Park City Firefighter Romance

Rescued by Love

Reluctant Rescue

Stone Cold Sparks

Snowed-In for Christmas

Echo Ridge Romance

Christmas Makeover

Last of the Gentlemen

My Best Man's Wedding

Change of Plans

Counterfeit Date

Snow Valley

Full Court Devotion: Christmas in Snow Valley

A Touch of Love: Summer in Snow Valley

Running from the Cowboy: Spring in Snow Valley

Light in Your Eyes: Winter in Snow Valley

Romancing the Singer: Return to Snow Valley

Fighting for Love: Return to Snow Valley

Other Books by Cami

Seeking Mr. Debonair: Jane Austen Pact

Seeking Mr. Dependable: Jane Austen Pact

Saving Sycamore Bay

Oh, Come On, Be Faithful

Protect This

Blog This

Redeem This

The Broken Path

Dead Running

Dying to Run

Fourth of July

Love & Loss

Love & Lies

ABOUT THE AUTHOR

Cami is a part-time author, part-time exercise consultant, part-time housekeeper, full-time wife, and overtime mother of four adorable boys. Sleep and relaxation are fond memories. She's never been happier.

Join Cami's VIP list to find out about special deals, giveaways and new releases and receive a free copy of *Seeking Mr. Debonair: The Jane Austen Pact* by going to this site - https://dl.bookfunnel.com/38lc5oht7r

Cami is the author of over a hundred romantic suspense novels. She is a USA Today Bestselling and award-winning author.

Hugs and happy reading!

cami@camichecketts.com

www.camichecketts.com

- facebook.com/CamiCheckettsAuthor
- twitter.com/camichecketts
- instagram.com/camicheckettsbooks
- amazon.com/Cami-Checketts/e/B002NGXNC6/ref=sxts_entity_l_bsx_s_def_r00_t_aufl?pd_rd_w=0B0n9&pf_rd_p=c227778c-e6e6-4d97-8a5a-0854898f1e10&pf_rd_r=DX4DYK796QAC0SEYFPV4&pd_rd_r=0edd556d-1ce2-4369-81c9-c8df05bebc93&pd_rd_wg=FJEth&qid=1573271538
- bookbub.com/profile/cami-checketts

ROYAL SECRETS - EXCERPT

Julia Adams stepped out into the lamplit street in front of the quaint cottage she was staying in and started into a jog. She could hear the waves past the thick hedge on her right. Hopefully she could pop through the tropical wall and out onto the beach soon. It was four a.m. and still pitch-black outside, but her internal clock was all messed up. She had spent over twenty-four hours in airplanes or airports, the last four in a puddle jumper with only her and the pilot, a handsome man named Treck who had an easy smile.

After an effective argument on her part, he'd confessed his connections to the hidden island of Magna's royal family. The confession had made Julia even more excited to meet the elusive and supposedly beautiful people. Treck kept her entertained with stories of his and the second royal son's exploits. It sounded like Prince Bodi Magnum had quite the inventive mind. At least the stories had kept her distracted as they flew over teal-colored ocean and she prayed the rattling, bouncing airplane would make it.

She'd landed after dark. A beautiful young lady, Zara Lancelot —apparently the royal family's assistant—had been waiting for her. She had taken Julia straight to the cottage that was only a few minutes from the castle and the other royal residences. Julia had seen the towering castle lights, the steeples of a church, and some town lights, but it had been too late for a tour. She couldn't wait to witness the exquisite kingdom with her own eyes.

Prince Bodi Magnum had contacted her brother's marketing agency and asked for a top executive to help him create and market trips to the island of Magna, known to the world as the Hidden Kingdom because of how private and secluded it was. The prince already had ideas such as a medieval jousting tournament and fair, beach and mountain exploration, and the charm of an entire country set in the past. Julia had begged until Justin had finally acquiesced and given her the job.

Now she was here and ready to explore despite the early hour. A run on the beach and a long shower and she'd be ready to evaluate and advise Prince Bodi. It was so magical here. She'd caught glimpses of the towering, well-lit castle and the old-fashioned lamps lighting the streets as the rickety plane had landed. Those same lamps now lit her way, but she really wanted to be on that beach. She could hear the waves rolling in now. Any minute now, she'd find an opening in the hedge. Would the sand be soft or hard-packed? A few pictures she'd found online that had leaked from the island showed lush mountain ranges, a gorgeous royal city, and farms and ranches scattered over the rest of the island.

Julia increased her pace as the pounding of the waves on the sand grew louder and her excitement mounted. She finally found a break in the hedgerow and darted through it onto the dark beach. She was blinded for a second by the lack of lamplight on this side of the hedge. She ran smack into a wall—a moving wall.

A wall of flesh and muscle.

"Oomph," she gasped as she rebounded toward the ground.

A hard body fell with her onto the sand. Warm, strong arms wrapped around her as the person rolled quickly and took the brunt of the impact. It was a matter of seconds before they settled in the sand. Julia was stunned, but she dimly realized she was cocooned in a man's arms. Her heart raced and her stomach gave a little lurch. Something about this man holding her was both stimulating and comforting.

"Are you all right?" a cultured, smooth voice asked.

"Um ... I think so. Did I take you out?"

The man chuckled easily. Julia's eyes adjusted to the dim moonlight and she was gifted with the sight of a handsome face, all manly lines, with thick dark brows and penetrating dark eyes. "I think I may have taken you out. I saw a shadow dart out of the hedge, but I reacted too slowly. Forgive me."

"Sure." Julia tried to move, but he held her so tightly that she couldn't squirm free. Part of her didn't want to be free, but she didn't know this man and she shouldn't want to languish in his arms. "Um ... excuse me."

"Oh! Forgive me again." He released his hold on her and jumped to his feet, bending to help her up. His hands remained on her elbows, tracing warmth through her flesh. He stared at her. "You're an outsider?"

She backed up a step and his hands fell away. Losing his warm touch was regrettable, but she wondered about his tone. Did he not like outsiders? Was he going to take her up to the volcano and sacrifice her for not fitting in? Nobody knew much about

Magna, but it was rumored that the Hidden Kingdom had some archaic traditions. She'd heard that the island's inhabitants were graced with olive skin and dark hair and eyes. Her red hair and blue eyes would definitely stand out.

"How'd you guess?" She forced a bright tone and prayed he wasn't the druid guardian of the beach, intent on keeping outsiders from invading his peaceful island.

She needed to stop reading fantasy books.

A smile crinkled his cheeks, creating nice laugh lines around his eyes and mouth. "I've never seen a redhead anywhere but on the television screen."

"Sheltered life, eh?" She tossed her long red ponytail. As a child, she'd hated the attention she received because of her coloring, but she didn't mind it now. It helped that her hair had darkened to a deep reddish brown over the years. "What do you think?"

His eyes trailed over her and warmed her all the way through. "It's beautiful," he murmured. "May I?"

"May you what?"

"Touch your hair."

She blinked at him. "I don't think we're that friendly," she said, though a large part of her longed to give him permission to touch her hair, her hand, or maybe wrap her up in his arms again. Her eyes had fully adjusted now, and she liked the lean lines of his arms revealed in his short-sleeved shirt.

He chuckled and said, "Forgive me. What brings you to Magna, Miss Red?"

She arched an eyebrow. Something in his eyes said he knew exactly who she was and why she was here, but he obviously wanted to tease her. "You've never met an outsider before, eh?"

"Not one as beautiful as you."

She wanted to accept his compliment, but his nickname from before still stung. "Well, here's a tip. Us outsiders don't like being made fun of for the color of our hair."

He gave her an alluring smirk that made her lean closer without intending to. "Even though we are 'not that friendly,' I should explain that I wasn't making fun of you but giving a compliment. You are undoubtedly the most beautiful and exotic woman I've ever seen."

Her dark-red hair garnered attention in America, but nobody had ever said she was "beautiful and exotic." She wanted to giggle like a teenager, but instead she said, "Nope, sorry. We are not friendly enough for you to give me an empty compliment." She flipped her hair over her shoulder and jogged around him and along the sandy beach. It was soft sand and slow going.

He caught up with her easily. "I hope I have the chance to become 'friendly' with you on your visit to our beautiful island." She couldn't place his smooth accent, probably because she'd never heard it before, but she loved the way he talked.

"Is this your personal island?" she asked, trying to discern his expression in the dim light, but it was harder now that they were moving.

He smiled, but his answer gave nothing away. "All Magnites feel this is their personal island. We're very proud of our beautiful country and our heritage."

"I see. And what are you doing jogging so early in the morning?"

"Patrolling for redheaded intruders."

She stared at him, hit a rock with her foot, and would have gone down if he hadn't reached out to steady her. His touch brought fire to her arm and she wasn't sure she was ready to be attracted to some local who was either teasing her or was a military sentinel of some sort. Gently tugging her arm free, she walked instead of trying to run in the thick sand. He slowed to keep pace with her.

"You're teasing me," she decided. "You don't actually patrol for intruders."

"I am teasing you," he admitted. "We have military boats who patrol for intruders. The closest island is a hundred and eighty two miles away, so it's rare we get curious teenagers coming by."

"Why are Magnites so private?" she asked. Some lights appeared to their left on the beach, another small cottage with warm light spilling from the windows.

"Magna used to be one of the wealthiest nations in the world because of the gold mined for hundreds of years from our mountains. In years past, we had to fight hard to protect our wealth and our people's independence and privacy. The gold has been gone for over twenty years now. We are still a fiercely proud people, but we lack the currency or military power to back it up. We have very little to trade because of our isolation and lack of shipping ability, but we are mostly self-sufficient due to our mild climate and hard-working people."

"That might be why I'm here," she mused. She'd had no idea Magna might be in financial trouble. "Prince Bodi asked me to come ..." Her voice trailed off as he glanced sharply at her and she realized the prince might not appreciate her spilling her purpose or ideas to some handsome guy on the beach.

"Prince Bodi asked you to come?" he prompted.

"I'm sorry. I don't know if I'm at liberty to say."

He gave her a slight smile. "We are 'not that friendly,' eh?"

She laughed, grateful he seemed so easy going. She probably should've been more leery on the beach alone in the pre-dawn hours, but this well-built man seemed protective, intriguing, and well-mannered. "No, we are not." They walked in silence for a few steps, and she saw some faint pinpricks of light up on a mountain peak. She couldn't wait for the sun to rise. Maybe she could get a tour of the island before her real work began. "Do you know Prince Bodi?"

"Very well." His voice was confident; he didn't seem intimidated by the prince at all. Was he military, truly patrolling for intruders? Maybe he reported straight to the prince and would inform him that his new marketing associate was loose-lipped.

"What's he like?" Treck had given her all kinds of stories and insight, but he was the prince's closest friend, in his words, so his opinion might be skewed. She'd like to hear from another local what the second royal son was like.

"He's incredible—kind, hard-working, smart, charming, handsome." He glanced askance at her, his eyes dancing with humor.

"Are you sure you didn't just describe yourself?" she deadpanned.

He roared at that. "I suppose all those characteristics could apply to me as well." He sobered. "Truthfully, Bodi's a good man and a good friend. I think you'll enjoy working with him on ... whatever you're doing."

"Thank you. I'd better ... get my run in and get ready for the day."

"Is this where you're intoning I should run back the other direction?"

She didn't want him to, but it wasn't smart to encourage him. He was attractive and appealing, but she wasn't here to meet a man. She was here to work, and maybe help this country more than she'd imagined. She loved the idea of rescuing them from financial doom. Julia Adams riding up on her white steed, saving the kingdom and the handsome prince. She smiled to herself. Just being on this incredible island made her imagine she was in a fairy tale.

"Does that smile mean you don't want me to run away?"

"I like to run alone," she insisted, though truthfully she would like more time with this handsome, intriguing man. The island was small enough that she was sure to see him again.

"I know when it's time to make an exit." He saluted her and turned the other direction. "Goodbye, Miss Red. It was a pleasure meeting your beautiful self this beautiful morning."

She turned and faced him instead of jogging away as she should. "The pleasure was all mine, oh druid guardian of the beach—or what should I call you?"

"Druid guardian of the beach is fine, but my friends call me PB."

"Peanut butter?"

He chuckled. "Yes, ma'am. Do you like peanut butter?"

"It depends if it's creamy or chunky."

His smile deepened those laugh lines that she liked. "Definitely creamy. I'm smooth and charming and *definitely* creamy."

Her stomach somersaulted again. She wished the sun was up so she could see exactly how deep brown those eyes were. "Too bad. I prefer chunky."

She whirled and ran off down the beach as his laughter floated in the air behind her. She smiled to herself. She wouldn't soon forget their conversation; what a warm and intriguing welcome to the country of Magna. She hoped she'd see PB again.